Of Seven Fir Trees and the Snow

THE GERMAN LIST

THOMAS BERNHARD

Of Seven Fir Trees and the Snow

Early Stories

Selected and translated by
DOUGLAS ROBERTSON

LONDON NEW YORK CALCUTTA

This publication has been supported by a grant from
the Goethe-Institut India

Seagull Books, 2025

All stories were originally published in German

First published in English translation by Segaull Books, 2025

ISBN 978 1 80309 545 5

British Library Cataloguing-in-Publication Data
A catalogue record for this book is available from the British Library

Typeset by Seagull Books, Calcutta, India
Printed and bound by WordsWorth India, New Delhi, India

CONTENTS

TRANSLATOR'S ACKNOWLEDGEMENT

The translator wishes to extend his sincerest thanks to flowerville for her invaluable insight and assistance in reviewing the complete preliminary draft of the translation and providing information for the notes.

The Red Light

Today's story will be an eerie tale for a change,* and perhaps from the outset many a reader's nose will be crinkling, because in our age there is no longer a place for this kind of thing, or at most it takes place in some distant corner of the world, say, Eastern Friesland, where certain people have second sight, and where one hears of advance warnings of lugubrious incidents. But this story here, which unfolded in this country of ours, is true, bitterly true, and there are plenty of people still living who can bear witness to thc following events.

It all happened thirty-four years ago, in the last month of the winter of 1916. February had brought in a great deal of fresh snow in those heaping amounts that are dreaded in the mountains.

Originally published as 'Das rote Licht' in *Salzburger Volksblatt* on 19 June 1950 under the name Thomas Fabian (*Fabian* being a variant spelling of the surname Thomas' mother Anna Bernhard assumed when she married Peter Fabjan, who then became Thomas' stepfather and guardian). [Trans. after Bernhard's editors]

* That is, presumably, in contrast to the usual content of the section of the paper in which the story appeared. [Trans.]

On the Mitterberg, at the foot of that line of pale limestone-faced ridges known as the Mandelwände,* stands the Arthurhaus, an inviting mountain inn. Here a stalwart, capable landlady, Mrs Radacher, resided alongside her husband. She kept both her feet firmly planted in reality; she had never been one of those brooding types who occupy themselves with abstruse ideas.

In any case, during this wartime winter she never would have had the time for such things, for every pair of hands had plenty to do then. Directly across from the Arthurhaus, in the Swiss cottage a mere stone's throw from it and separated from it only by the deep rift valley, a company of ski infantrymen in training had recently been quartered and were still residing. But the commanding officer of the company, a first lieutenant, had along with his subordinate officers taken lodgings at the Radachers' abode, so the woman could hardly complain of a lack of work to be done.

Each day, with the help of their ski instructor, the soldiers practised their runs on the training ground, on the pastureland that steeply sloped down from the Mandelwände towards the stonework Swiss cottage. The ski instructor was an experienced man; he knew his way around the mountains, and he was also much better versed in meteorology than the

---

* The Mitterberg is a mountain in the Untersberg, a portion of the Berchtesgaden Alps straddling the German state of Bavaria and the Austrian state of Salzburg; the Mandelwände are perhaps so called because of the resemblance of their faces (*Wände*) to slices of almond (*Mandel*). [Trans.]

commanding officer, who was a city person. The mountain dweller had not liked the weather of recent days at all. He found the abundance of fresh wet snow well-nigh eerie.

On the morning in question, that of 18 February, Mrs Radacher was extremely busy in the kitchen. When in the course of her work she briefly stepped out in front of the house and looked over at the Mandelwände, she could not believe her eyes. She noticed a red light whose peculiar lustre was pouring across the white snow of the pasture like something magical and not quite real. She rubbed her eyes. Was she dreaming in broad daylight? Was she hallucinating? No, everything she was beholding was distinct and tangible. The pasture was glowing a deep red like that of the eternal flame of the sanctuary lamp in church. Then Mrs Radacher fled back into the house in terror.

She hastily told her husband what she had seen. He laughed her to scorn. Then the two of them peered through the window, but the red lamplight had gone out. And yet the woman could not manage to calm down. Was some great disaster impending—perhaps an avalanche on account of all the fresh snow?

She returned to her work in the kitchen and forced herself to think of other things. But she could not shake her mind free of her apprehension. At lunchtime, her food did not taste right to her, and she found it hard to wash the dishes afterwards.

Time and again she gazed across the rift valley at the Swiss cottage, at the pastureland beyond it. Then, all of a sudden—the light was there again! It spookily spread across the snow, causing it to glow blood red.

She screamed. Her husband hurried to her side, but by then the light was no longer to be seen.

That evening, the ski instructor was sitting with the officers in the Arthurhaus' public room. He briefed them on the condition of the snow and expressed concern. In view of the weather situation, he strongly advised them against going to the training ground the next morning.

The commanding officer demurred. 'Duty is duty,' he said. 'Our comrades are facing the enemy himself, so we are obviously obligated to take a bit of bad weather on the chin.'

'But in this case there is a chance of an avalanche, sir,' retorted the ski instructor, 'your entire company is in danger.'

At this moment Mrs Radacher entered the room. She had heard the words just spoken by the ski instructor, and she could no longer contain herself. She *had* to tell the gentlemen what she had seen; she had to be capable of persuading them to vacate the Swiss cottage. She plucked up her courage and asked them if they would be so kind as to listen to her without laughing at her.

They all gazed at her in astonishment. Then she gave an account of her experience; she warned, implored, complained.

The first lieutenant smiled to himself. After the woman had left, the men gazed at him in anxious anticipation. Everybody noticed that he was struggling to reach a decision. But he quickly made up his mind. Only a few minutes earlier, just after the ski instructor had finished speaking, he had been on the point of finally yielding to the 'reasonable arguments' the latter had adduced. But when the woman had come in afterwards with her strange story, his honour as an officer had bridled against giving credence to such ramblings. Now there could be no question of his acquiescing, of his yielding under any circumstances!

'Old wives' tales!' he said dismissively. 'Tomorrow morning, the company will report for duty and exercises on the training ground as usual!' With these words he stood up and left the room . . .

The morning of 19 February dawned. The company in the Swiss cottage were roused from bed as usual; the day's schedule began; the hours of duty were announced. The ski instructor did not show up; a substitute took over for him in leading the athletic exercises. The first lieutenant was also absent.

After breakfast, the entire company marched out. Only those who were ill or had office duty remained behind. The company moved into the training ground.

And then the horrible event happened. The avalanche came, and there was no escaping the implacable force of nature. The colossal masses of snow buried the entire company beneath them and also blanketed the Swiss cottage. Only upon reaching the deep fissure that was the rift valley did the devastating convulsion come to a standstill. The Arthurhaus remained intact.

The recovery work began. Here and there a man was rescued unharmed or pulled out in an injured condition. But of what significance was this compared with the mighty harvest death had reaped? No fewer than fifty-eight men had had to lay down their lives. Their bones rest in the cemetery in Bischofshofen.

The Settlers

They had come home in the same transport, *they* being the eighteen-year-old Rupert, who no longer had any relatives, and Ferdl, who was about a year older and whose mother had died in the war, so that he was now as much alone as his comrade.

For two weeks they shovelled sand at a building site in town; then at Ferdl's suggestion they went to work for a farmer in the country; at least the meals were heartier there. They slept in the hay barn, and because it was springtime, they were none the worse for this. In their free time, they roamed around the countryside. In the course of these rambles, a patch of uncultivated land between the forest and the moor kept catching Ferdl's eye. 'We could settle here,' he said, and sucked on his pipe like an old man.

Soon they began working busily on the little piece of ground in the evenings and on holidays. The two of them weeded, dug, and carried stones, posts and planks to the spot. The place was isolated, and their activity remained hidden

---

Originally published as 'Die Siedler' in *Salzburger Volksblatt* on 8 September 1951 under the name Thomas Fabian. [Trans. after Bernhard's editors]

from view for a long time. By late summer, the hut, or, as they called it, their house, had all four walls and a roof. Soon they would be able to move into it. And they had also staked out a parcel of earth for gardening; it was, after all, untilled soil, unclaimed land.

Upon awaking from their first night spent under their own roof, they found the forester standing on their doorstep and asking them from whom they had received permission to build there. He said that he had been observing the whole project for some time and that he was pleased to have an opportunity to speak with the 'masters of the house' at last. They replied by meekly asking whom the land belonged to and averring that it was after all untilled soil. To say exactly who owned the property was not a particularly simple matter, opined the forester. In any case, they would need a permit from the local government.

When after several futile meetings they finally managed to see the mayor, they received some bewildering news. He said that the property itself was an entailed estate, but that, upon the estate's dissolution under the auspices of the international administration of Austria, it had fallen into the hands of new, foreign owners, whose heirs had bequeathed it to the local government in exchange for a promise never to revoke their right to hunt on it. That a sublease from the local government would not be possible. That in the absence of any contact with the heirs no kind of provision could be made. The two youths calmly returned to their dwelling. A few days later, two men dropped by and asked to see the building permit and the certificate from the building commission. Oh, so they had no permit or certificate to present!

Eventually, a gentleman from the tax office showed up; he asked to see every possible kind of document, checked their identification papers, took notes; he rattled off all sorts of terminology and phraseology that neither of the lads could make head or tail of.

The idyllic solitude of their little hut on their uncultivated patch of land was now history; at all hours of the day they were visited by people who, on the authority of brusquely flourished credentials, would po-facedly avail themselves of their right to interrogate the youths. They were subpoenaed by various administrative bodies, and the farmer, their employer, really became quite vexed, because both his labourers were absent from work all too often on account of official business. Rupert and Ferdl no longer felt at ease within the walls of their settlers' house and eventually came to prefer sleeping in the hay barn again.

Meanwhile, there arrived a thick envelope containing an eviction order that, in artfully chosen and peculiarly hifalutin words referring to all sorts of legal paragraphs, asserted certain things whose upshot, as near as the two settlers could tell after long perusal of the document, was that they had lost the right to hold onto the fruit of their labours.

So Ferdl and Rupert's dream of having their own little patch of earth had received a rude awakening. They continued working on the farm, and when winter came and it grew cold, they started spending their nights in the cowshed.

A Big-City Afternoon

I'm not exactly sure any more, but I was looking for the sun somewhere. I knew that there was such a thing. And that kept me on my feet. But what was imparting the most strength to me was my youth. I had only (or already?) traversed twenty years. A wonderful period, perhaps an excessively beautiful one. 'The more captivating your memories are,' I thought, 'the more arduous the present is.' Life struck me as most odd and yet 'lively'.

For three days I had been staying here, in a big city. We were a million people, all different and yet basically the same. I saw them every day, indeed, every hour, and only the night like a miracle ever drew a veil over this concentrated world. Each and every day there were five hundred or a thousand faces that I walked past. And behind each of these faces a different mystery was hidden. There were broad faces, narrow

---

Originally published as 'Von einem Nachmittag in einer großen Stadt' in *Salzburger Nachrichten* on 13 December 1952 under the name Thomas N. Bernhard, with the N presumably standing for Nicolaas, Bernhard's official first name (Thomas being his official middle one). [Trans. partly after Bernhard's editors]

faces, round faces, pale faces, puffy faces, cheerful faces, child-like faces, terrified faces, blasé faces, stupid faces, and faces that seemed to be made out of nothing but flesh and a revolting slurry. Those of this last sort had lost all trace of expression. They lived for their own sakes. I still have quite a vivid picture of them, those 'flesh' faces.

I found it very strange, the city. And hour by hour this strangeness metamorphosed into a ruthless coldness. Was it perhaps even hostility? Last night I dreamt that I was embracing an ancient oak tree and that I could feel it breathing . . .

The shrill braking of an automobile yanked me back. From behind a car window a contorted face threatened. Rings glinted on thick fingers; a hefty neck protruded from a suit. A man's voice shouted loudly and threateningly at me from behind. The automobile vanished around the corner. A giant cloud of gas absorbed me. For a few seconds I believed in death . . .

The song of the streetcar tracks was steadily crescendoing. I felt their tremors beneath my feet. The sound was thrilling, infinitely hastening. Somewhere a train howled. Small dogs barked promiscuously at one another and the nauseating voice of a woman meddled in their barking. I counted the kerbstones, the large ones and the small ones; then I noticed the doors and windows, a hundred, two hundred of them. There were so many.* A tangle of wires spanned the gap

---

* See the following autobiographical passage in *Wittgenstein's Nephew*: 'For whole weeks and months I have a compulsion, whenever I take a streetcar into the city, to look out of the window and count the spaces between the windows of the buildings along the route, or the windows

between me and the vastness. I reminded myself of an animal trapped behind the bars of a large cage. And I walked and walked, farther and farther. And over everything smoke from the tall, rigid chimneys hung in the yellowish-grey sky.

I had no goal. I had been trying to get to know the city for eight whole days. There were quite a number of street intersections that reminded me of toys from earliest childhood on account of their lights that flashed red, yellow and green at brief intervals; there were some small parks. There were six or maybe ten trees standing in the grass there. Everything was well tended; everything fitted in with the surrounding area. The little shrubs with the red flowers were numbered. A small sign was nailed firmly to their tender trunks. The numbers on them were quite high, far higher than a thousand, because the city was large, indeed, a city of more than a million inhabitants with many parks. Slowly, I began to understand a great many things. Noble narrow gravel paths crisscrossed the green. I walked along a row of iron-mesh chairs. And again I noticed the faces; they were just like the others. They were narrow and pale and evincing a great deal of 'spentness'. Decrepit old women were being pushed along past me in wheelchairs. And the city? Its din continued unrelentingly; any interruption of it seemed unthinkable. It was merely somewhat muted, somewhat remote.

---

themselves, or the doors, or the spaces between the doors; the faster the streetcar travels, the faster I have to count, and I feel I have to go on counting until I am almost demented.' (Thomas Bernhard, *Wittgenstein's Nephew: A Friendship*, David McLintock trans. [New York: Alfred A. Knopf, 1989], p. 89.)

I sat down and took a rest. Perhaps I even needed to sleep? Not for the first time I raised my head and . . . suddenly a heftily built woman was standing directly before me; she was grinning through half-rotten teeth and had a fluttering double chin. With her right hand she was rooting about in one of her nostrils; her left hand was rummaging through a black leather purse.

'Sixty groschen, sir!' she said and held a white slip of paper up to my eyes. Her mouth opened; her eyes were staring at something infinitely distant.

For a moment I did not know what was happening, but then I dug into my pocket, searched in it for a long time, was disappointed and irate at the same time to find nothing, stared into the red face with the long hair, stood up hastily and left. I thought I could hear a term of abuse being flung at me; then I walked across the gravel with my hands clasped behind me and suddenly I was standing back in the busy street, with all those people and the red, green and yellow lights that reminded me of my earliest childhood toys . . .

Of Seven Fir Trees and the Snow . . .

A CHRISTMAS FAIRY TALE

Every year on Christmas Eve I would walk the long walk over to St Brigid's* in order to fetch the nativity candles for our Christmas table from a white-haired, kind-hearted woman. 'This one is for protection against fire, this one is for protection against adversity and this one is for eternal life,' the old woman would say before wrapping all three up in a linen rag and sticking them in my little bag, which I carried on my back. Then she would give me a few sugar-sprinkled crescent moons and stars, smile and shut and lock her front door while I trudged back home through the deep snow . . .

Originally published as 'Von sieben Tannen und vom Schnee' in *Demokratisches Volksblatt*, a Salzburg-based newspaper, on 24 December 1952. [Trans. after Bernhard's editors]

* Probably the Filialkirche St Brigida, a church in Henndorf am Wallersee (the Henndorf mentioned in paragraph 3), a small town in the Salzburg area near which Bernhard lived as a child and where he was introduced by his grandfather to the playwright Carl Zuckmayer, who wrote a highly favourable review of his first novel, *Frost* (1963).

What follows happened exactly seven years after the world had taken charge of me.

I still had a good hour to put behind me to get to Henndorf, which lay in a broad valley which extended all the way to the lake and in which it could get so cold that even the frost-traced flowers in the windows would die of exposure. Not long after the sun had vanished behind the hills, the moon was already wandering above the dark spruces. Every now and then, a light from a room in a house would emerge from the plain of fog or a crow would caw from the edge of the iced-over pond. The crystalline snow crackled under my firm footfalls, and my breath turned to steam in the moonlight. I swelled my lungs and counted the stars that were lighting up in the sky, but in the end there were so many that I no longer knew where I had started counting and where I had left off. On the white expanse of infinite extent at the horizon were mirrored a million terrestrial suns that thus combined to form a single light that shone upon the entire world.

At that moment I may very well have been thinking about heaven and about all the people who didn't believe in it. At that moment I may have been very happy and content and hearkening to thousands of things that were within me and all around me: the deep night!

And when I looked up at the treetops and still farther and farther upwards, I also realized that eternal life, the same eternal life that the old woman told me about, was the most exalted of all sensations in the eyes of Being . . .

I stopped in front of the little chapel with its painted Madonna. And because I always paid her a visit when I was passing by, I beat the snow from my shoes and stationed myself beneath the deep blue vault. I clasped my hands, but I did not pray, for when happiness and revelation are so close by, one simply has faith and submits. Three saints were standing there behind the iron railing: the first in a gold cloak, the second in a yellow one and the third in a brown one. All three were made of centuries-old ash wood. Their partly merry and partly serious faces had been blanched by the sun. But the longer I contemplated them, the larger they became. Their hands began to move; their eyes lit up, and after that it even seemed as though they were speaking with one another. Perhaps even the railing sprang open? But a choir of hundreds of angels was singing . . . I slowly followed them as they walked, through the icy winter, ever deeper into the silence of the night.

The three saints led me to the outskirts of the woods, where the newly fallen snow lay so deep that only the very tops of the young firs were visible, and where everything was so calm that nothing could be heard but our footfalls, those large, dark holes being pressed into that white blanket. From time to time one of the sagging boughs would tremble, or snow would fall from the branches as though a deer had just stepped into the clearing. Here and there a star seemed to crackle. The Great Bear shed thousands of flakes of dandruff onto our heads . . .

'Come,' said one of the saints, 'we are on our way to the seven firs that signify the world.'

'The world?' I asked.

'Yes, the entire world . . .' affirmed the shortest of them, whom I knew to be named Anthony; and the third one was already far ahead of us.

My footfalls grew lighter and lighter, and eventually I was soaring like the moon above the entire vast wooded area.

'This way!' said Andreas, who had a wondrous face and deeply luminous eyes. I was astonished that he was unaffected by the cold, for he was still wearing nothing but a pair of thin-soled sandals on his feet. But his beard alone seemed to keep him quite warm enough . . .

In the midst of the snow, not far from a short hill, stood seven fir trees. The first was the tallest, the seventh the shortest of all. They could scarcely remain standing for all the snow that was weighing down their tops.

'There they are . . . ,' said one of the three men, 'all seven of them. They live very retired lives, Beauty, Truth, Purity, Reason, Faith, Hope, and . . .'

'. . . and Love,' said the shortest man, to whom the moon was being rather unjust in shining on his baldness.

'Love fares the worst of all of them—it just can't catch up with the rest,' all three of the saints said pensively while shaking their heads. Then there was complete silence.

'Why can't it catch up?' I asked after a while.

'Well,' they mused, 'because . . . because it's so sickly . . .'

'It should be nurtured by somebody. After all, there are people who know how to tend to it,' I asserted in genuine astonishment.

'Nobody takes the trouble to minister to its needs. Nobody has any time . . .'

'Any time?'

'Yes . . .'

'Ah,' I said, 'then perhaps it will waste away . . .'

I shook the tree so roughly from all sides that all the snow fell from its frail boughs—and then I felt as though it were taking a deep breath.

Truth leaned forward. But Hope, which was almost as short as Love, was at that moment illuminated by the moon in such a way that one might have thought it was made of unalloyed gold.

Everything was wondrously beautiful beyond all measure.

But the three saints stood there and were at a loss what to do. All four of us were sinking deeper and deeper into the snow, and every now and then, and without lessening their lustre, the oldest saint would pluck down from the sky one of the stars and warm his hands with it. And at length I cried out in downright rapturous enthusiasm: 'Then I will nurture it! I will . . .'

A heavy hand had fallen on my shoulder. My father was standing behind me.

'What have you been up to all this time?' he asked, and his breath was warm and ascending like down into the night air. I meditatively walked down the narrow pathway with him.

'Are you cold?' he asked.

'No . . .'

'And what is this thing you intend to nurture?'

'Love, Father . . . Hope and Love . . .' I whispered, and of all the people in the world, I was the happiest.

Crazy Magdalena

'. . . Yes, yes, I knew her quite well. She came from our village. Her father was a postman and owned a small cottage with two goats and a fat pig that he would slaughter before Christmas. What is more, we were in the same grade at school for a year. We also used to go carolling together, but even by then something insidious was lodged behind her strikingly blonde tresses. Nobody ever knew exactly what she was thinking. On one occasion our teacher gave her a resounding box on the ear.

'Those were good times.

'But she was basically a good-natured creature who gave away everything. On one occasion, she stationed herself before the front door of her house—I must admit this happened some thirty years ago—and threw her playthings into the crowd of laughing children who were just then coming out of the church. And she vehemently refused to take back her dolls and stuffed donkey, her cooking spoon and colourfully embroidered scarves from the children's dumbfounded

---

Originally published as 'Die verrückte Magdalena' in *Demokratisches Volksblatt* on 17 January 1953. [Trans. after Bernhard's editors]

parents. Because of this, a fair number of people in the village thought she was not quite normal, and scrutinized her long chain of ancestors—which contained nothing but farmhands, maidservants, railroad tie-layers and a wastrel—in search of somebody they could have said definitely had a screw loose. But they discovered no such person and contented themselves with "Crazy Magdalena".'

My friend raised his eyes. He could tell a story well when it was getting towards midnight, and now one could hear the distant singing of the streetcar as it strained its way through the black city walls. From time to time a bell rang, voices wafted up from below, or a pane of glass at the front of the restaurant across the street rattled. He came to see me often, and on account of his natural way of living I quite liked him. And then, too, perhaps he had been drawn to this city of more than a million souls by something similar to what had drawn me to it. He was perfectly happy with his métier as a painter, as a painter of works of art, if I must put it that way, and he understood to a turn how to combine his painting—the initiated either termed him an impressionist or had no idea what to make of his pictures—with his night job as a parking-garage attendant. Here as there he held his own. When he was being a painter, nobody ever would have guessed he was a parking-garage attendant; when he was being a parking-garage attendant pulling in barely 110 schillings a week, nobody ever would have guessed he was a painter with good innate technique and even better prospects. Even though he sometimes had quite uncommon if not insane views about life, its days and nights, its ascents and descents, and could never be persuaded to budge an inch from this extravagant 'insanity' on any point, we were still the best of friends. This became unmistakably evident a few times each week, most especially when we borrowed money from each other. I liked to drink a glass of apple juice and he, perhaps for the same life-beautifying reasons, liked to make a side trip to the tobacconist on the quayside to pick up some cigarettes, those pernicious little white sticks with which he subsequently befouled the already heavy air. Admittedly, he beheld fantastic dreams in the blackish-yellow haze of smoke . . .

'She was about twenty-five years old,' he continued, 'when I saw her in Paris. The postman's little daughter, the crazy creature with the old-fashioned underclothes and the compulsive urge to give things away, had turned into a dancer, a beautiful woman who rode along the Champs-Élysées to the theatre every evening in a freshly painted limousine. She danced to variations by Brahms and Debussy. I was dumbfounded by the thought that a girl who knew nothing in the world apart from the churchyard, the lady who ran the general store and the cross-eyed schoolmaster—who indeed knew nothing about anything; nothing about the world of hatred, of low cunning, of madness, of mawkishness, of the world of stupidity, of war, of slander, of avarice—could possibly be transformed into a woman who ranged between red plush armchairs and the no-less-flattering-than-dubious odours of *A Thousand and One Nights* as though she had grown up immersed in blue smoke and the rustle of silk. I had a brief interview with her. Her comportment was off-putting and strange. She had turned into an obnoxious fixture of the international urban scene.

Her eyes were instinct partly with hunger and thirst for the hanging gardens of the modern Semiramis, partly with ambivalence, sorrow and despair. Her eyelashes fluttered, and after ten minutes of sitting face-to-face with her, of drawing closer to her as she drew closer to me, of feeling her out, I found myself beholding a doll conversing with the tips of its long white fingers, incessantly twitching its ears as though it formed a part of a mechanical system . . .'

'And how did she fare as an artist?' I asked.

'Well, she certainly must have worked hard. She could dance marvellously. When you were watching her from the gallery, you would have had no trouble at all believing she was some kind of higher being. The gold on her body, the supple rhythmic movements of her pliant, glassy hips, radiated something singular but decidedly disagreeable . . .

'The next day, the critics' columns were brimming over with excessively zealous superlatives. I even saw her picture a couple of times. I bought the newspapers . . . I brought a whole stack of them home with me and showed them around . . . but as I was saying earlier, as chance would have it, I was in Paris of all places. I was staying somewhere in that sea of houses in the students' quarter along the Avenue de Neuilly. I produced a couple of good sketches and sold them. I was wishing I could live there.'

'And what happened next?'

'Next . . . ?'

'With Magdalena . . .'

'Ah . . . it was quite peculiar. I hadn't heard anything about her in a long time. I had even forgotten about her. You forget about beautiful women when they don't have anything special going for them apart from their beauty . . . say, an appreciation of painting . . . or motherhood. In the meantime, I did a ton of living. I worked and lived for the most part in the city. In the summer, I travelled back home. My father died, and then so did my mother . . . But life kept moving along. A fair number of things from that time would have been worth writing about, perhaps even all of them would have been, but calamities always got the upper hand, and often my first glimpse of a day of sunshine was enough to consume me with bitterness. You see, my worries, my worries about how I was to earn my daily bread, were unending. And why should it even have been otherwise? I felt as if I were only just hitting my stride in the kind of life I have pursued ever since, the life of a painter.'

We both laughed, but ours was no ordinary laughter; it was, rather, the laughter of two men experiencing every possible walk of life in a big city. To be sure, he was roughly twenty years older than me, but I fancied he was in the same frame of mind as me anyway.

'Somebody or other procured me an exhibition of my works in one of those coffeehouses that are to be found all over the city. I had just finished a couple of new paintings and two well-made woodcuts.'

'And did she come to the exhibition?'

'Yes . . . all of a sudden she was standing there . . . on the first day there were only seven viewers, total strangers . . .'

'Did she speak to you?'

'No, she ran away from me! I caught up with her in the street. I was almost run over by a car. She was weeping bitterly. Her beauty was gone; it had simply flown away . . . she had some still-valuable rings on her fingers, but her clothes were filthy. Her face was sickly and emaciated. It was enough to shake up anybody.'

He stood up, lit a cigarette, and blew small clouds into the warm air.

'I walked with her to her tiny one-room apartment. Everybody had forsaken her, you understand, everybody. Her friends! Even the affluent factory owner's son from Marseilles. She had so many men . . . she led a life of ease. Back in Paris, she already gave the impression that she was ill. Twice she was put into a sanatorium for a lung disease. Her dancing days were over . . . Apart from the doctor who called on her every week, she no longer had any other human being in her life but me.'

He paused for a moment.

'Shortly before the end she was planning to return to our village. "I loathe this world!" she had exclaimed. She had become as poor as a beggar. But when she died and her coffin was being driven to the cemetery, I really thought to myself that a queen had died, an uncrowned queen who had experienced exactly as much good fortune as misfortune in life . . .'

'Yes,' I said, 'and that's what she was . . .'

'And we all love life . . .'

We stood up and he went downstairs to resume guarding his garage while I stayed there and counted the figures on the wallpaper for a long time and thought about Paris, which I had still never seen . . .

The Legacy

She ran down the hill, down through the trees, past the sign reading 'Grocery'. She stumbled over a plank. Her shoes were soaked.

'Come . . . quickly . . .' shrieked Ottilie, an awkward thirty-year-old creature, 'she's dying . . .'

The puddles kept dividing; her shoes kept splashing straight into the middle of them; she couldn't catch sight of them in time; with every step she trod into uncertainty, quite without forethought, yet sharply and forcefully.

'Everything's coming to an end for her . . .' stammered Ottilie. Rose could barely stomach the word 'end'.* What was coming to an end? A life? What sort of life? The life of

---

Originally published as 'Das Vermächtnis' in *Demokratisches Volksblatt* on 21 February 1953. [Trans. after Bernhard's editors]

* See the following passage from Bernhard's 1978 play *Immanuel Kant*: MILLIONAIRESS . . . Tell me Professor Kant / what is the basis of our more or less permanent fear of death / our dread of the end / KANT (*flying into a rage*). Don't say the word end. (Thomas Bernhard, *Save Yourself If You Can*, Douglas Robertson trans. [London: Seagull Books, 2024], pp. 239–40) [Trans.]

Theresa, the old schoolmistress with the gold-rimmed spectacles. The good old woman with white hair . . . it had been springtime when she was still walking, tramping with a stoop, across the burgeoning meadows, her head cocked slightly to one side. Rose could hear her voice, could feel her warm hand, her peculiar, fitful breathing . . .

'Up there!' ordered Ottilie. They ran up one of the village's many long, narrow flights of stairs. All of them creaked the same way, had the same handrails, the same smell . . .

The walls reeked of putrefaction and apples, of dampness and pigs . . .

When they got to the narrow door, they saw Anna, the dying woman's sister, emerging from the house.

'Shush!' she hissed, 'shush . . . quiet . . .'

'Is she going to die?' asked Rose.

'Yes, she's going to die . . . in an hour . . . or maybe later today, or maybe tomorrow . . .'

'What has she been saying?' inquired Rose.

'She's been saying she wants to die right here and now . . . she'd rather not wait even another day.'

The three female figures did not stir. The fragrance of candles sat on their foreheads, as did the fragrance of flowers, of skin, the stench of sweat, pears, pollen . . .

'What has she been thinking . . . ?' asks Rose.

'Thinking? Her? She hasn't been thinking anything.'

'Is it very painful?'

'What?'

'Dying,' said Ottilie in a subdued and peculiar tone.

'Dying?' asked Anna. And then she seemed to be pondering the question for a few fractions of a second. And her eyes took on a look of fascination; they were like the eyes of a hunted animal that in the midst of the despair of a winter night sees a light shining . . .

Inside, the old woman was lying as if in state, exactly as though she had already been dead for a few hours. Her face was illuminated by a single candle. Somewhere on the wall Rose saw a shadow . . . she held a finger up to her lips. No cry came from her chest—just a long-drawn-out hideous note.

And then they went in. It was no corpse that was lying on the bed with stiff hands, an equally stiff head and squinting eyes. The old woman stirred.

'Who's there?' she asked. A thousand-fold loneliness cowered in her eyes.

'Who's there?' rang out a second time, more loudly, peremptorily.

'Rose . . .'

'You?'

'Yes, Miss Therese.' She said '*Miss* Therese' because she had never known her as anything else. She had taught hundreds of people how to read, write and do sums.

'How is it going, Rose?'

'Well, Miss Therese.'

'Enough of the *Miss*,' said the excruciated voice. 'I am a dying old woman . . . I won't live another day. I am already, as everybody will say, "gone".'

The old woman sat up. She made a hand gesture. Rose drew quite close to her.

'Are you happy?' asked the old woman.

Rose nodded. Whereupon the old woman gently shook her head.

'I am no longer anything but some kind of . . . ' said the dying woman suddenly, 'no longer anything but a stone falling into the water . . . can you see that, Rose?' she said tenderly. 'Don't I hear bells ringing . . . ?'

She was breathing as sparingly as she could, but time was melting away beneath her sweaty fingers. Her chest seemed to be paralysed. The world . . . Grab hold of it one more time and crush it in your hands . . . Now, quickly . . . but everything she was clutching at was turning to ashes. Her heart was beating right on up to the end, after seventy years . . .

She had something else to say.

'You must surely want to have a child,' she said and pulled Rose all the way to the bed.

'It's the most terrible thing in the world when you haven't got a child . . . when you've reached the end, your last day, and there's no child standing and weeping at your deathbed . . . '

She sank back onto the bedclothes. 'Can you even understand me?' she snapped. 'I have known you since your first day . . . the school, do you still remember it?'

'The class . . . '

'Yes, the class . . . you were bitterly poor; that was why I adopted you, took you in as I would have taken in a helpless creature . . . and also because you didn't have a mother . . . '

Rose wept without knowing that she was weeping. And then they laughed, and then they wept again.

'You really became my child . . . ' the old woman imploringly insisted. And Rose nodded.

'One day you will learn that the older a person gets,' she cried, and tore at her shrunken breast, 'that the older a person gets, the more beautiful life becomes . . . at bottom . . . but I am dying . . .'

The two other women stepped back. They could hear the clock ticking, voices beneath the windows. A peculiar whispering . . .

'If you can't have a child, you mustn't be unhappy about that, not you . . . you are young.' Her voice failed her. Rose propped up her head, shoved the pillow under it.

'Listen,' said the old woman. 'Adopt a child, a poor child . . . but do it completely, do you understand? Then I shan't be worried about you. No child is strange to us . . . and yet . . .' Her eyes suddenly lit up, as if they were the eyes of a young woman, even if the twilight of death was passing across their pupils.

'Then I shan't be worried about you . . . a woman who hasn't had a child hasn't lived . . . Having a child means having everything.' Her breathing was laboured; each time she inhaled or exhaled, the room was filled with a lyrical sound, a curious draught. It smelled of medicine, of bodies and roses . . .

'Rose . . .'

'Yes?'

'. . . always be a good person, and be brave . . .' She closed her eyes. 'Be brave,' she whispered. The three women waited; they waited, but they heard not a single further word from her lips which were now merging into her slowly and uncannily expiring face; those lips which were now submitting to the laws of this earth, like everything that has a name, a title, a good will or any meaning whatsoever in this world. Rose kissed the schoolmistress' forehead. A wondrous world was coming to an end with her, but a new, perhaps even more wondrous world was dawning. The room was swelling with the sound of children's voices . . . with the peals of bells . . .

The three women gazed unblinkingly at one another. They soundlessly took their first steps back into the new world; they listened and listened into the distance, into some faraway somewhere, but heard no reply . . . not that day, not the next.

The Poorhouse of St Laurin

From the poorhouse, which had been standing at the top of the hill there for centuries, there ran a footpath leading to the broad street that stretched all the way to the centre of the big city—and from there you could find your way to anywhere in the world. Once you had put the ancient gate behind you, you would find yourself standing outside in fresh air and you would behold the sky, which at times was more beautiful there than elsewhere. The nuns would say their prayers in the garden, and the old men would chat with the old women about the young world. They had been doing this for many years, and when they woke up in the morning, they would behold this world with their bloodshot eyes and reflect how lovely it would be to behold just a little longer those trees that were sometimes white with the pollen that the wind would waft their way in May and June, the pollen from those sweet blossoms hanging on the peach trees and cherry trees.

Originally published as 'Das Armenhaus von St Laurin' in the newspaper *Salzburger Volkszeitung* on 10 October 1953. [Trans. after Bernhard's editors]

Most of the old people there were like wizened trees that stooped under the force of tempestuous winds and refused to accept that someday soon they were going to be cut off like a piece of wood to be burnt to ashes. They tried harder and harder to stoop slowly and equably in the hope of finally reaching that brilliantly scintillating water of purity that they had thirsted for since the first day of their lives. And in the evenings they would sit on the benches in front of the St Laurin poorhouse, and their old heads were white like the crowns of the young cherry trees when the sun shone on them . . .

A couple of years earlier you would have also heard the whirring of a spinning wheel from time to time—but you didn't hear it any longer, because on a certain spooky night the old woman who had worked its treadle from morning till evening had died without having bequeathed her secret to anybody. Everybody had been very sad at the time, and two of the old people tried to work the abandoned spinning wheel's treadle—but they couldn't manage to. From that point onwards, nobody in the house knew how to spin cloth, and so day after day the sheep's thick fluffy whiteness kept piling up, and nobody knew how to deal with it. In those days, there was also an old man who had whittled clogs out of ash wood for the other inmates of the ancient house. When he died, quite suddenly, there was some wood left over, along with a pair of clogs that he had begun making, and the others shook their heads and whispered peculiar things to each other. After that you would see all the old people sitting on the house benches, embroidering and knitting, thinking and singing, and a number of them looked exactly as though they were thinking about nothing but their approaching death . . .

But there were also lots of people outside the poorhouse, an entire world beyond its old door, through which a person walked every hour, and you never would have had enough time to count all those people out there or even to make their acquaintance. There were good people and bad ones, poor ones and rich ones. You could look at some of them and at others of them, and eventually you no longer knew exactly which of them were actually poor and which of them were rich.

The street that ran down from the poorhouse into the metropolis was full of destinies. In that street, there were many thousands of heads which appeared in the window frames every morning, young heads and old ones, blond ones and brunette ones; and in each of these heads something was happening. But none of them knew what was happening in any of the others', much as each of them would have liked to know. But all the people there had a business, a profession, a job, something of some sort to do, a calling for which God had placed them in the world; one knew more or less what their individual destinies required of them . . . The man from the liquor store, who lived at the end of the street, spent his entire life selling nothing but plum brandy and wine and liqueurs and in the evening he counted his money, after he had lowered his grey rolling shutters. The baker's apprentice rose at three in the morning and went to bed at six in the evening, and his mother was in bed by four, because she was ill and had brought a lot of children into the world. Then there were also tailors and carpenters, teachers and porters, shoe repairmen, actors, sandal makers, postal clerks, warehousemen, bricklayers, paper hangers and streetcar conductors, hospital nurses and train-car cleaners. There was also a pitiful junk dealer who always coughed when you held out your hand to him, and who had a daughter who was very beautiful and on whose happiness he had pinned all his hopes—until he died . . . Many of these people spent their entire lives standing in the street and digging up dirt, chipping concrete and pulling handcarts full of quicklime, handling buckets on broad rooftops, operating cranes, standing with wet feet in the gutter, crawling around in dark unwholesome ditches and therefore being badly paid and despised . . . and so nobody was very much surprised when one time one of these people just went and emptied his bucket of water onto the head of one of the others, threw down his pickaxe, pocketed his pay packet and vanished; when one fine day he just resurfaced with his body sunbrazened and covered in scratches, with wildly unkempt hair and a mind deranged* by the world and by thousands and thousands of worthy thoughts that he could never dispose of because he was despised—and he walked, onwards and onwards—and finally jumped into some ditch somewhere amid the grey rows of houses, so that nobody could ever discover a trace of him again, apart perhaps from a waterlogged shoe, a shirt, one of his identification papers, on which was

---

* *Deranged* is my rendition of the original's *verstörten*, a word closely related to *Verstörung* (*Derangement*), the original title of Thomas Bernhard's 1967 novel known in English as *Gargoyles*. [Trans.]

written what he had been called, what had been oppressing him and what, in his heart of hearts, he actually was . . .

The poorhouse was very old and so was the world on its doorstep, including the big city. Sometimes the people here seemed even older than the poorhouse and the city combined. They were all sorry that there was no longer anybody in the house who might have spun the cloth or whittled the clogs. They no longer did much of anything, because their lives were over. They simply stood just outside the gate and waited to be let in . . . they queued up one right after the other. Most of them were still there pretty much solely for the sake of discharging the greatest of all earthly duties—dying. Some of them died beautifully here and others of them died hideously. But once they were dead, they all looked as if they had spent a lifetime in one another's company, and as if they were all brothers and sisters . . .

There were so many of these brothers and sisters. They all had but a single mother, a great, good sun, and a father, the earth, and a handful of good fortune and a handful of guilt, nothing more . . . Together they comprised a veritable family, the old and the young, the ones standing outside and looking in through the windows, the poor and the rich, born or unborn . . . And all the while both those inside the poorhouse and those in the world on its doorstep kept wondering who could once again work the spinning wheel's treadle or whittle clogs or do anything else to impart some joy and variety to the time that continued to march steadily past . . .

Great, Inconceivable Hunger

One time back then, in those forsaken and yet ever-so-unforsaken days, I was walking along the street. I watched the birds on the rooftops and the people beneath the sky. I sniffed at the doors and at the windows and thought about how the trees here were all of roughly the same height—just like in the distant city of gold on the far side of the Blue Mountains. Slowly I turned towards the grey facades of the houses which were wrapped in music, in the distant secret music of my childhood, in the days and hours beneath my grandfather's trees and in the gardens near the green river.

The dead are good people, I thought. Then amid the thousands upon thousands of little stones here, on the damp ground of the city of ghosts, I searched for a reddish-brown stone like the ones that number in the millions upon millions in my native city.

This is a translation of a version of the story 'Großer, unbegreiflicher Hunger' that was originally published in the 1954 instalment of the annual literary anthology series *Stimmen der Gegenwart*, edited by Hans Weigel. A different version was published under the title 'Der große Hunger' [The Great Hunger] in *Demokratisches Volksblatt* on 15 October 1953. [Trans. after Bernhard's editors]

The beauteous city!

There are poets who sing its praises, the praises of its lustrousness and meekness, of its breezes and its towers, which graze the sickle of the moon on summer nights.

The city of ghosts!

I thought about the people I had seen during the day. I had roamed eastward, westward, northward and southward; their faces kept rising from the depths of the gorges of loneliness; imbued with the fragrance of the chestnut trees, they kept crossing the path of my gaze; the pain and the thousandfold sorrow of life propagated endlessly.

On the bench in the park, I became conscious of the loneliness of my heart, the loneliness of my flesh and of my blood, of my bones, the loneliness of my young soul which was wandering about aimlessly by both day and night and was unable to find repose.

I didn't know if I would ever again see the beauteous city on the far side of the Blue Mountains. My father had grown up in it and died in it, and more than once, hundreds and thousands of times. My father had spoken there and so had my mother; in the course of the year, the peach tree in front of our house had grown two or three new branches—it was a happy time. All this, I thought, is something that I would like to experience one more time: the voice of my father and the voice of my mother. I would like to experience the sunrise and the sunset, the open skies over the verdant countryside which always ends with the river in the west but begins each day with the sun in the east.

I pulled out the last letter I had received from the beauteous city and read some of it. I always began afresh from the beginning. My cousin Michael's oversized handwriting pounded away at my brain like a hammer, but by and by I was gripped again by my old great yearning for my reality, for the Blue Mountains and for what lies on the far side of them.

'We are now harvesting the fruit,' I read in my cousin's letter. 'The apples are finer than last year's. We are overjoyed. They are rosy-cheeked and bigger than ever before. This morning, we went to church and prayed.'

I paused, contemplated the tree.

Later, I read further: '. . . I plan to send you some lard. You know of course that things are not going well for us either, but we still have lard, yes, lard . . . I am praying for you . . . Your cousin, Michael.'

And at the very bottom of the page: 'Don't forget to put on your scarf at night. You know that's important. Your mother always used to say that.'

After I had risen from the bench, I took out of my coat pocket the schilling that I had found early that morning. I held it up to the sunlight. I pulled out my handkerchief and polished it. I looked at the sower and at the field and I looked at the Blue Mountains far beyond them.

Slowly I walked along the gravel path and watched the park warden as he fed the pigeons, threw more and more crumbs into the crowd of pigeons, crumbs over which they were squabbling the way human beings squabble with one another over every breath they take from the very beginning.

Once I had reached the long street with the yellow and red lights, I began thinking about home. But this thinking vectored towards another world that seemed unattainable and failed to procure me the strength I would have needed in order to survive the moment. I had nothing—nothing but the long road, steps and walls, wind and loneliness, train lines, women, girls, and a hunger that a man can feel when he wakes with a start and cries out a name that he knows has been stricken from the great table that spells happiness for him—when he wakes with a start like a wild animal.

I had been meditating for a long time; then at length I entered a 'gourmet' grocery store. I went up to a man whose upper lip was slightly trembling. The man's entire body seemed to be a single incurable illness.

'Haven't you got anything for me to do?' I asked. 'I'm out of work, but I have to live. I'm not choosy. Have you really got nothing for me to do?'

And then I thought to myself that there is a moment at which one calls it quits with everything, including the Blue Mountains, including the towers of the fair city, and retains but one desire: to run away as quickly as possible.

'Across the street, somebody is feeding white bread to the pigeons,' I said to the man.

I gazed into his oedematous face, which kept pulling itself apart and pushing itself back together—into this dim-witted, pulpy circular face whose eyes seemed to have been implanted in it at some kind of eye factory.

Later, at a vegetable stall, I again asked: 'Haven't you got anything that needs to be done? I'm not choosy.'

The man at the vegetable stall rolled his eyes. He said: 'Clear away that stuff over there for me! That pile of rotten leaves! I'll give you some of my tomatoes. They're not quite fresh any longer, but they haven't quite gone bad yet either. If you're hungry, you can eat them—otherwise I'll throw them out.' He turned his back on me for a moment as he continued: 'I always have something left over for a poor devil. I am a good Christian, do you understand? So get on over there and clear away that stuff for me.'

He rummaged through a crate of tomatoes with his puffy hands.

I now turned to the half-rotten tomatoes, to the brown, slimy leaves. I saw the oozing tomato pulp, around which stinging flies were circling. One time I cast a glance at the person behind the tomato crate—then at the pudgy, busy feet of stout, laughing women. I saw roaming shopping bags, roaming bread, roaming hams, roaming sausages, cheese, butter, milk bottles—everything was roaming past me, vanishing before I had taken it in. Bleak midday hung over the big city and weighed heavily on its houses from which the sound of cutlery clattered out into the thick air.

'Here they are,' said the fat man. He sneezed, rubbed his nose, despised me in my entirety as I was.

'Now get lost,' he said: 'if my wife sees you, you'll get clocked on the head.'

Soon I was walking and eating tomatoes, fruits of the earthly paradise,* fruits from *A Thousand and One Nights*, imbued with a slight smell of putridity, with a whiff of the south, touched by that man's oedematous hands, picked perchance by healthy, robust Italian girls. I stuffed my belly full of fruits; I swallowed them one after another; I gorged myself until it almost hurt. Soon I had only a couple of the red hemispheres left in my sack which was already soaked and brittle in many places and on the verge of falling to pieces.

My knees ached. In the midst of my great, instantaneous tomato-induced bliss I suddenly felt like a man who has fought in a war right up until its end and is now returning home and does not know where home is; like the men in the ragged uniforms of a defeated army; men creeping along on stilts; men with swollen bellies, emaciated chests, battered arms, broken-up hearts.

I suddenly remembered that I still had the schilling in my wallet. For a schilling I can buy two rolls or a glass of milk, I thought. Milk? For a schilling? But I had no desire to drink milk in the big city, because its milk smelled of metal, of machinery and centrifuges. I craved milk from the udders of the cows back home, with the scent of the grass and the singing of the milkmaid to go with it. And as I experienced the sensation of the tomatoes in my belly and the sensation of life as it is endured by all young men of our time, I saw my

---

* Perhaps Bernhard evokes paradise here because a tomato is sometimes called a *Paradeiser* in Austria. [Trans.]

mother, my good departed mother, walking above the tall trees, with a benevolent smile on her countenance.

'Don't forget to put on your scarf,' she had always said.

I forged ahead.

I pressed the doorbell-button of a metropolitan 'mission' into its outer wall. I saw the stern face of a woman, two piercing eyes; I heard a voice. I entered. Soon I was sitting in a broad armchair facing a large desk. Somewhere the hour hand of a clock was tracing its path. I heard the plonking and jingling of typewriters. Into the mouthpiece of a telephone receiver the woman was unremittingly saying: 'Yes . . . no . . . yes . . . no . . . yes . . . no . . . yes . . . but . . . no . . .'

This went on for a long time, and her face indistinguishable from millions of other faces scarcely changed at all.

It had got quite late when she said to me: 'What do you want?'

I told her the highly unremarkable story of my life. I knew it by heart; I no longer needed to rehearse it in my mind. I wasn't embarrassed—no, I spoke calmly, but for all that, my voice was imbued with a great sense of dread.

The oldish woman seemed highly suspicious of me.

She ran the tip of her pencil over her white sheet of paper: 'When? How? What? Why? That? No! You? Ah . . . Are you crazy? You do understand me, don't you? . . . Do you understand me? Perhaps . . . Do please pay attention . . . In my opinion . . . Don't you understand me? Can't you understand me? . . .' I was drowning in this torrent of words.

Nobody in the big city noticed that I was hungry and young. I said so many, many times, but nobody listened. I knocked on many, many doors, but nobody opened any of them.

I hungered for everything: for apples and pears, for butter and honey, for mountains and for fields of grain, for birdsong, for river waters and for the sky over my loneliness, for maternal women and for age-mellowed fathers, for gardens, footpaths, prophecies, for all the fruits of the earth.

When I got back to my room, I put the remaining tomatoes in the drawer of my table. I couldn't eat any more of them; I could only cast my gaze through the window and onto its frame, onto the stone quadrilateral against which my thoughts were chafing themselves raw, the square onto which my soul was slowly bleeding to death.

'Where is the beauteous city?' I asked myself.

'Where is the green river?'

And nobody brought me an answer.

Then came the evening, the night.

'Why?' I asked myself. 'What for?'

I threw myself onto the bed. I tried to fall asleep. But I kept seeing the four walls, a towel, an old table, a typewriter, a pair of old shoes. I saw a door and a window and behind them the Nothing.

I shut my eyes. Nobody in the world slept a sleep like mine at that hour. I saw the homeland of the homeless, the infinitude of the finite, the heaven of the earthly, and the eternally ripening acres of apparently fruitless human beings.

A Winter's Day in the Mountains

Since the very first days of my life I have felt at home there. Detours compelled me to leave, but my hopes and worries kept coming back and urged me to return: to return to the landscape of sylvan pathways, to precipitously plunging torrents, to the solitude of a mountain village. In winter, it is the snow that casts an imperishable spell on man who leaves behind everything by which he is otherwise confined amid the burgeoning houses of the city, where life is unrelentingly buried hour after hour and one's good ideas are trodden flat by the muck of a bitter existence between walls with whose cracks one has been well acquainted from time immemorial.

You are well acquainted with the morning, when the canopy of clouds dissipates and the fog ascends above the frozen pond. You are well acquainted with the tree that stands hunched outside your window. You are well acquainted with the village. And when you step out of the centuries-old gate in the shadow of the church tower and take a breath, the world that lies behind you is one that you have never loved.

Originally published as 'Wintertag im Hochgebirge' in *Demokratisches Volksblatt* on 13 January 1954. [Trans. after Bernhard's editors]

But when you now walk, walk onward with a swift, vigorous gait, as your fathers and grandfathers walked, wretched and immersed in the bitterness of existence, as tillers of this landscape who were nevertheless wise to the mysteries of the sunrise, you are struck by its simplicity. Everything is simple; the whole of life is simple and grand.

You walk to the cemetery, your collar turned up, your cap pulled down over your ears, and trudge your way between the graves. There lie your brothers and sisters, covered in metre-thick snow, and the little roofs atop all the crosses are full of jollity. Nothing has anything to do with mourning. When a person dies here, he nevertheless remains a part of our little community. They don't just bury him in some field for the masses; no, they carry him out and pay their regards to him every Sunday when they go to church. For all their poverty, the people in this area—mountain farmers, cottagers, shoemakers and other artisans—believe in the fruitfulness and resurrection of Creation. And when in church they sing along to the playing of the organ, and their warm breath ascends into the icy air like fog, when the altar boys ring their little gilded bells, they all feel: we are not alone in our solitude.

What pains you here is that although you are rediscovering your native land on this path, the people here regard you as a stranger. They can see: he isn't wearing a coat made by our tailor. He isn't wearing any kind of hat that we wear. He has different shoes. He has a different face . . . and then you greet them as they greet you; you stick your hands in your trouser pockets as they do. It is too late. You are no longer one of them. You have become different. Who made you into who you are now? Why have you become like this? you ask.

The path passes through the village and leads up to the mountain. Here stand ancient suntanned wooden houses. Within them you see little children pressing their warm noses against the frost-work on the window panes in the morning. Did you also use to do that? And then you wander along the glitteringly silvery tracks left by the sleighs that have preceded you uphill along the same path. You feel like a newborn, as though your life had been completely pointless until now. The brook at the edge of the path is steaming and rippling below; it is overhung with snow. As a boy, you used to take a running jump and leap over it—and back. No, you can't do it now. Why can't you?

The little hay barn is the same as it was years ago. A long time has passed. Back then it was summer. If you step up quite close to the shed, you can smell the fragrance that seeps through its cracked beams. You often used to spend the night in a hay barn when the night took you by surprise. You didn't use to worry about having a bed. It made no difference to you. You must have been very young.

You can wander for hours here without encountering a human being. People would force themselves upon you during the war. There were too many people who were worried about you, who wanted something from you, who scrutinized you, investigated you, who forced you into their ranks, who soundly thrashed you because you didn't play along. It was a bitter world brimming over with human beings. And so you would get anxious in their presence. But here not a human soul is to be found, only every now and then, a hundred metres from you, a deer steps into the path, stands still and waits, beautiful, noble, in the divine snow-covered landscape, and if you approach it, its eyes look at you as if they had just opened for the very first time.

Now the sky is clear above the mountains. Now you behold the powerful living rock; your gaze wanders over a hill on which larches from which a shower of gold once fell are growing . . . On one side the Heukareck casts its mighty shadow across the deep valley through which the railway, which you cannot see, meanders;* on the other, the Hochkönig towers into the blue. But this is enough as it is: don't describe anything, just behold it. As surely as the flowers of summer are destined to blossom namelessly before your eyes, the snowy landscape of the mountains is destined to show itself.

After putting three hours of snow and ice, splitting trees, wooden footbridges and hay barns behind you, you espy a house. The hue of its wall is barely distinguishable from that of the snow. Its roof is white; its clothesline, stretched between two trees, is hung with laundry that has frozen solid. In front of it a young woman is sitting in a sleigh. Perhaps she has never left this place. Cocooned in wool, she greets you with a laugh, runs up to you and goes with you into the

* In his memoir *Die Kälte* [*In the Cold*] Bernhard writes of his 1949–51 residence as a patient in a tuberculosis sanitarium with a view of 'the six-thousand-foot Heukareck, the unscalable rock-face which to me became a symbol of fate'. (*Gathering Evidence*, David McLintock trans. [New York: Alfred A. Knopf, 1985], p. 296) [Trans.]

house. Before entering, you knock the ice from your frozen shoes, take another look back at the path that you've just come from, but the fog is already cloaking it near the firs. A Christ Child could have actually flown in here a few days ago . . .*

'Isn't that right?' you ask.

The girl nods. They are sitting in the front room, in the midst of their poverty. The mother is cutting slices of home-baked bread from a loaf; the father is warming himself at the stove. Did you venture out into the cold? they ask, and the question makes it obvious that they regard the city dweller in their house as a weakling. Venture out? They for their part toil away to their last breath, haul wood down from the mountains through the snow on weekdays. A harsh life. They have little: a roof over their heads and butter and milk, and with childlike eyes they peer into a calendar diary that you bring them. They spend their entire existences working up here, in seclusion—their cries are inaudible even at the nearest farm—and they mostly die on the mountainside, under a tree trunk, rarely in bed; but the mothers do die there, because they bring their children into the world in solitude.

The journey back is long and the night takes you by surprise. By and by you see the stars. They shine above you and beneath you shines the snow. You feel cold. From time to time you are alarmed when a branch snaps, when a bird screeches,

---

* An allusion to the infant Jesus as the Santa Claus of German-speaking countries, and an indication that the narrator's visit takes place shortly after Christmas. [Trans.]

but by and by the village lights are shining towards you, and just like in the old days, years ago, you walk downhill along the well-trodden trail. Although you are hungrier here than you have ever been anywhere else, night-time in the mountains, this 'being left entirely to your own devices' on the darkly shimmering earth, still imparts to you an intimation of endurance and eternity.

The Decline of the West

My cousin's prophecy had emphatically failed to be fulfilled. Not only was it not raining, but the skies were blue above the rooftops of our little town on Saturday. In a clean linen shirt, with a prayer book under my arm and with my head held a bit higher than usual, I walked up to the old parish house. It was there that I was to receive from Father Zephyrin Kiderlen my final instructions on how to conduct myself on the forthcoming Sunday.

After the priest's fat cook Marie came to the front door and let me in, I sauntered across a plush purple carpet towards the priest's distant study.

'Softly,' whispered Marie.

She was responsible for maintaining peace and order in the house.

'Knock twice,' she said. 'On the outer door and on the inner one. And be decent enough to bow to him.' She said this and more as though I were setting foot for the very first time in

---

Originally published as 'Der Untergang des Abendlandes' in *Linzer Volksblatt*, a Linz-based newspaper, on 17 July 1954. [Trans. after Bernhard's editors]

this peaceful, palatial house which was seldom visited by a soul apart from me, a couple of other people and, at certain times—but never before the harvesting of the pears from the tree that hugged its wall—by the archbishop in his purple robe.

I knocked.

When I was commanded to enter, I opened the door and poked my heated head into the room. My gaze sought out the priest, who, as always at that time of day was sitting behind the high back of his upholstered chair, although today he was reading not a newspaper but—and this was what in particular caught my attention today—a big book: *The Decline of the West*.*

No sooner did I sit down than I yearned to know what sorts of things might be contained in this strange dark book, to know why it was as thick as my mother's cookbook, and above all, where in the world this West that was its subject happened to be located.

Father Zephyrin Kiderlen, to whom I had greatly endeared myself over the preceding few weeks, cleared his throat.

'The West is here where we live,' he said, 'in contrast to the East, through which, as you of course know, Jesus Christ,

---

* The established English title of Oswald Spengler's two-volume treatise on the philosophy of history, *Der Untergang des Abendlandes* (Vol. 1: 1918, Vol. 2: 1922). Kiderlen is evidently reading one of the two volumes, as the first one-volume edition (an abridgment) did not appear until 1959. *Abendland* (literally 'evening land') more vividly preserves the connection between the Occident and sunset than *West*; complementarily, *Morgenland* (literally, 'morning land'), the term by which Kiderlin refers to the East in the original story, is more evocative of sunrise than *East*. [Trans.]

the son of God, roamed after he had arrived in the world to redeem the souls of men and women . . .'

I had already heard about all that. And about the olive trees and the cypresses, about the Virgin Mary, Bethlehem and a bunch of other things on the banks of the Jordan. But nobody had ever before told me that I lived in the West.

'The West stretches from the East across the Mediterranean to the Far North,' said the priest.

He took something out of a strongbox.

Now I wanted to know why this place, which to the best of my knowledge had both things—namely, a west and an east of its own (not to mention a north and a south of its own)—was called 'the West' of all things.

Zephyrin Kiderlen, whose sister sang the most peculiar songs to her own plodding accompaniment on the organ every Sunday, took his pipe in his hand and packed its brown bowl with aromatic tobacco. 'This tobacco,' he said, 'comes from the East, from somewhere not far from Jerusalem.'

He lit the pipe.

'Our region of the earth,' he continued in his gentle voice, 'is known as the West, because the sun, after it has risen in the east in the morning, sets on us in the west in the evening.'

This made everything completely clear to me.

'You of course know where the sun rises in the morning and where it sets in the evening. Or do you not know? Over there, where it rises, is the east; over there, where it sets, is the west.'

I nodded.

The priest savoured his pipe. He sucked on its shiny mouthpiece, and each time he did this his cheeks were drawn inwards. When he blew out the smoke, they turned red like two apples shimmering in the early morning sun.

'And what's in that big book?' I demanded to know. 'Can so much really be written about this West?'

The old man in the black coat could not help laughing out loud. He could not even help coughing. He started choking; his face turned beet red. I sat motionlessly across from him with my hands in my lap. Then my gaze glided slowly and meanderingly over the mountains of books that were piled up on every side of the room.

Has all of this been written by people? I thought. By clever people? By poets, by . . .

Now I demanded to know why exactly this learned man whom I had never even heard of before had given his book the title *The Decline of the West.*

'Is this West really declining?' I asked. I feared the worst. I clasped one of my knees firmly with both hands.

Zephyrin Kiderlen took his pipe out of his mouth and drew a deep breath. 'Yes, and if it keeps declining, it will go under. Definitely! And it won't take much time to go under. And everything that crawls around on its surface will go under along with it—'

I sat in total silence. Now nothing whatsoever suited my fancy. Quick as a flash, I said: 'Then of course I'll go under too, and so will everything else, the entire countryside, the villages, the cities, my chapels, Elizabeth and the cherry tree on the hill, the deer in the forest and the frogs . . . ' I asked him how this West of ours could just go under one fine day, meaning overnight, and how it would happen to go under, and how soon we would have to deal with this incredibly bizarre business of going under . . .

The priest sneezed. He did this in a quite peculiar manner and fashion, more genteelly than anybody else I had ever met; there was even something about his hand gestures . . . His name was Zephyrin Kiderlen and he was our priest, a brilliant man, the most brilliant man in the parish, a man who reported directly to our father in Heaven.

'The connections are all internal,' he said. 'And what's happening internally, inside of us, so to speak, you can certainly feel, but you won't understand it until much later. Your time is still to come, in contrast to mine, which is almost over–but when it comes you will be a reasoning human being . . .'

He coughed.

'But let me give you an example,' he resumed, 'When a ship on the ocean, no matter how sturdy it is, has too much cargo in it, and this cargo is unevenly distributed, then this ship—in conformity with the laws of physics—inevitably declines and goes under; it sinks. That's what the West is now—a sturdy, overladen ship.'*

---

* Here Bernhard explores some of the semantic implications of the concept of *Untergang* embedded in the title of Spengler's book. He resumed this exploration nearly thirty years later in the 1983 novel known in English as *The Loser*, whose original title, *Der Untergeher*, translates most literally as *The Man Who Goes Under* or *The Sinker*.

'Hence the title *The Decline of the West*,' I said, although I had understood only a small part of the sage's speech.

Zephyrin Kiderlen gently nodded.

The room became dead silent. Not a single bird was singing outside, at the window—nothing was stirring; Zephyrin Kiderlen sucked on his pipe, breathed between puffs and gazed gleefully at me through his spectacles.

'It's a philosophical book,' he said. 'The man who wrote it is very smart. He is a thinker.'

I immediately thought of the old professor whom I occasionally crossed paths with on the street, an extremely peculiar person who hardly ever said anything and whom I had basically always regarded as nothing but a fool, because whenever you saw him he had his nose buried in an open notebook for the purpose of jotting something down.

'He is a philosopher—and he's also not a philosopher at all,' resumed the priest. 'His name wouldn't mean anything to you, like most names. There are men who have a mind magnified and sanctified by the Almighty. For them what they see is life, an estate, a house that is pleasant to live in; for them, it is a tiny cog in the giant machine of the world. Using the teeniest and tiniest bolts they build the world . . .'

By this point my mind had reached its limits. I nodded a couple of more times as the priest continued speaking, but in the end I had to admit that I had understood pretty much nothing the priest had just said. I had retained in my memory only a single word of his brief speech: knowledge. And even regarding that word I didn't know a thing; I hadn't the faintest idea how to begin thinking about it.

'Will a person really know everything,' I asked, 'once he's read this book?'

Eyeing me contemplatively, the priest leaned back.

'Nobody knows everything,' he said. 'The man who wrote the book, some years ago, doesn't know everything either.'

'But then,' I demanded to know, 'will a person know what's inside the book once he's read it from its first to its last page?'

Zephyrin Kiderlen took his pipe out of his mouth, coughed, and shook his snow-white head to and fro.

'Well, you see,' he averred—he kept moving the pipe farther and farther away from his head—'one person will know, and the next person won't. People are diverse. One person's brain has received God's benison, and the brain of the next person hasn't, as I have already said. A tricky business, Christoph. Even among sheep, there are only a few that can bleat in conformity with the rules of their art. Most of the people who have read this book don't know what's inside it. It exasperates them. God knows why. Most human beings, I tell you, are a vexation to books! Of course they pretend they understand what they're reading or have read and think themselves clever and wise and let themselves be taken in by perfidious perfumery—but as a rule they don't understand a blessed thing—and for the longest time their lives have been as limited as those of the women who keep stalls at the Naschmarkt!* And the most dangerous of them are those who give the appearance of knowing something, of understanding

* The famous food market in Vienna.

something. Most good books'— here the old man, using his pipe, indicated a number of them on the walls of his study—'never seep into the brains of their readers. They "don't set any bells ringing", as people say in our valley. Everything that is unsurpassably beautiful goes to the dogs. And whatever is unsurpassably beautiful and precious is also—mark my words—unsurpassably inconspicuous. That's the way it is with everything on God's green earth, my son. That's the way it always has been, from time immemorial. That's the way it always will be, my dear Christoph. Reading a book is exactly like praying. One should do both of them on one's knees and with devout attentiveness. Today's world is much too loud, too cunning, too unstable; people are lazy and idle and too wishy-washy to linger in the company of a book as it deserves. Books, my son, are little worlds unto themselves. When one opens them, one can walk around in them as long as one likes without getting boxed on the ears anywhere by anyone. That is what is so beautiful about books. And such worlds still exist in our time, worlds whose mornings are cloudless and whose skies are broad, and in which the sun shines eternally . . .

At this point, the aged priest concluded his speech. He picked up the book *The Decline of the West* and rotated it in every direction a couple of times.

'I always smell them. Each of them smells different, better than the next one,' he said.

Then he stood up, took a couple of steps, and shoved the big, dark, mysterious book into some place in the wall of books next to the window.

'The important thing is to summon up the courage to step into the worlds of books as if you had just arrived in the world and had never seen anything ever before. You've got to wander through their first few pages like a newborn, and then you too will perceive the fresh morning breeze as it wafts towards you . . . ,' said the priest.

I opened my mouth and pricked up my ears.

'Most people,' resumed the old man, 'no longer see anything. They bleat all over the place like our local sheep, sniffle like dogs, trumpet their platitudes to every point of the compass, wear beautiful dresses and coats, drink their coffee at punctiliously scheduled times and flock to wherever everything tastes sweetest. Mark my words, Christoph, wherever everything smells best and tastes best, you must don your hat—if you've got one by then—and vanish!'

I now felt as though I had understood every word the priest had said. This feeling came upon me just like boundless enlightenment pouring down from heaven. A new world was opening up, a land of unbounded beauty, a land without end.

'Perhaps,' opined the priest, 'some part of what I have just confided to you will stick to that white skull of yours. You will reward me for it. Most people nowadays smile at the pronouncements of an old man . . .'

He opened the little door of the stove that heated his study, knocked out his pipe, and gazed out the window.

'Life is like a treasure chest. Everybody can take whatever he likes out of it,' he said. Then he glanced at his watch, paced a couple of steps up and down and stopped. Shortly afterwards he remarked that I would have to be in the church in half an hour and that by then he would already be sitting in his confessional . . .

The Landscape of the Mother

There is only one landscape that man can truly love: the landscape of the mother. Wherever in the world I resided, restlessly pursuing my own path, a path beset by horrors and terrifying intimations of death, through the thousands upon thousands of nights of the metropolis that was a forlorn adolescence, the maternal landscape loomed.—

It is always its gently curved hill that affords me a view of the valley of peaceful farms, a view of the meadows and summer fields towards the dark, mystery-enfolded trunks of the fir forest. There is your homeland, you think to yourself, and you stride forward light-heartedly over the brittle fissures of the present age, enfranchised from the ailing worlds of the uneasy distance. Nothing in the reverberant streets consoled you. They did *not* squeeze you into the overcoat of their bygone-ness.* You still falter at many a turn in the path, but

---

Originally published as 'Der Landschaft der Mutter' in *Handschreiben der Stifterbibliothek* no. 13 (Salzburg, [August] 1954). [Trans. after Bernhard's editors]

* The young playwright in Bernhard's 1980 play *The Goal Attained* similarly says: '[My parents would] slip a jacket onto me and say / this is the

not a single worthy thought can be traced back to them now. You are all expectation; you keep wondering: is the tree there still young? Is the pond there still deep? Are the apples there already ripe and sweet? Do they already have everything, the rye and the wheat, in the house? Is she, your cousin, still *there* of all places?

The most beautiful thing in life is undoubtedly homecoming, returning home to the land of chapels, milking tables, trailing blackberries and the consoling sun. How often bitterness clings to you; you still owe some person a truthful utterance, some animal the protective stirring of your hand, your mother your thousandth thanks and your native land your love. But you can find nothing more conciliatory than the little piece of the world belonging to your parents, where you took your first steps from one thing to another, from the little kitchen garden to the azure shore of the lake.

All of a sudden you are realizing that everything is growing old; you, too, are out of time; the great hours of Being Here are crowding in on you. Your life is one great act of passing by, of passing by flowers in bloom, passing by clear and turbid roaring waters, passing by mystical sitting rooms full of wine and smoke beneath ceiling beams of the lofty centuries preceding your first breath. To track down meaning, to surrender to what is within *you*, with all your heart; this is your own version of change, your Up and Down between morning and evening; and this is your creed.

---

jacket you'll be wearing for the rest of your life / and I'd slip back out of the jacket.' (*Save Yourself If You Can*, p. 345) [Trans.]

Life is useful in the struggle it affords, but today you must knuckle down more seriously than ever so that you can remain the way you are and the way your forebears wanted you to be. Dangers lurk in your world, in all places, within and without, and the dances of the modern age are dances of death, and its images are images of the dead, and its music is a requiem. Therefore, I say, cherish the rustic's heart in your breast, and don't let anybody rob you of it. Be on your guard and remind yourself of the great duty you assumed on your very first day, when the mechanism of the clock in your mother's bedchamber also enclosed you in its powerful rhythm.

Beauteous is the landscape behind the hill. Between Seekirchen and Sieghartstein, beyond the mighty castle yonder on the hillside, lies your unforsaken world. Henndorf* in the Salzburg District is the isolated native town of my father and mother. Here their tuff-block house is still standing, with a garden in front and a garden in back. How many pieces of fruit have been carried into this house; how many coffins have been carried out of it? The House of Generations of Farmers; that is what I will call it. It has steadfastly outlasted countless ages and countless wars. From it have emerged farmers, craftsmen, poets, and painters; straightforwardly stout-hearted men and women who tilled their *own* fields. Each of them had a righteous heart and a cheerful disposition, the needful portion of seriousness, two strong hands,

---

* For Henndorf, see 'Of Seven Fir Trees and the Snow' (p. 14, footnote). [Trans.]

and a sound and alert intelligence. In the churchyard farther uphill, their names can be read and their stories seen.—

The sun still rises in the east over the sacred and already aged landscape. The hens still cluck, the ducks still swim down from the carpenter's house to the mill in the meadow. The children still laugh from the sitting-room windows; the trees still cast shadows on the highway; the cider still smells tart to us in the evenings. This village is more than a homestead and resting-spot to me. Its inhabitants are genuine human beings. They create, pray and haggle; they say sensible things. Often, too, one of them ends up a failure; then he drinks his fill and drunkenly falls into his grave. They are good with pigs, and with horses and cows as well. They know how to bake fritters and how to sweeten pears just the right amount. They are mistrustful of the new 'learning'. They don't allow themselves to be duped. There are blockheads in every community; why should there not even be some here alongside the Roman road? But by and large they are a pithy people. The springs on the borders of the village rejoice in a single unbroken existence shared with the larks in the rye fields.

How heartily I enjoy being with the farmers in the evening and climbing up to the church and listening to the songs of the choir and inhaling the incense! Rambling by myself through the churchyard in the fog, speaking with my people—this gives me strength. For they, the old people under the ground, have not died; rather, they have long since risen anew in jubilant splendour to till all the fields in the area with the blessing of heaven. As long as the farmer keeps sowing the grain and the farmers' wives keep rocking the children to sleep with the help of fine melodies before nightfall, we need not fear for the world.

An Oldish Man Named August

This happened back in the days when the great disruptive events of my life still held sway over me. The war, the loss of people and landscapes dear to me, still gnawed at my heart. It was necessary to find a way out of the tenebrous ravines of a half-opened adolescence, an exit from the darkness, to make a pilgrimage to that patch of light that shone through the remaining joints of the labyrinth and into my embittered inner world.

'Travel,' people had said to me: 'you must travel! There is mystery is to be found in a change of place, in moving forward, in the rolling of wheels, in the rocking of a jam-packed railway carriage . . .'—and so I packed my little suitcase and soon the front door of our old house was shutting behind me.

It was like a last farewell that segued into another one on the streets leading to the train station. I bade farewell to the rooftops, to the trees, to the shops of diligent small-town merchants who understood how to place their flesh-toned paper dolls at the most eye-catching angle, who ate roast on

---

Originally published as 'Ein älterer Mann namens August' in *Tages-Post*, a Linz-based newspaper, on 14 August 1954. [Trans. after Bernhard's editors]

Sundays, and who, when the sun was shining, made pilgrimages to the rural landscape at the foot of the mountain range to sit down in the grass with their newspaper. I wanted to salvage whatever portion of this night's phenomena that could still be salvaged, and I sucked in the walls, which were full of dank odours; I sucked in the fragrance of the ripening crocus in the city park, which was carrying me away with it, and I was transplanted into the savage horrors of my lost childhood, in which foreign apples had been picked from foreign trees, and which had been so full of adventures between evening and morning—so full of conquests and discoveries, full of terrifying incipient intimations of death and full of awakening love—that it wrested tears from my eyes.

I had boarded the train hastily. The door clicked shut; the long vehicle set itself in motion; the lights outside were engulfed by the gloomy hills; the rooftops sank into gentle hollows; unflaggingly, ever-more forcefully, the train was sucked into the distance; soon it was racing along the lakeshore, and finally it drilled into the inexhaustible west with undreamt-of rapidity.

My compartment was already occupied by four people. I placed my suitcase in the netted luggage rack and seated myself in the only available spot remaining, a corner spot that afforded a view of the dimly lit passageway.

I was tired. The preceding day had made me sleepy. In spite of everything, I began, like most people, to study the faces of my fellow-passengers, to analyse them, to assign them to specific walks of life.

Across from me sat a fat woman. She was sleeping; her hands were pursuing a downhill path along her lap, on which lay a bold-faced newspaper page. She might have been the wife of a washing-machine salesman, hence a woman of property. Her face was broad and watery; her hands pudgily glistened. Immediately beside me, a gentleman in a suit of the latest fashion was snoozing; he was young and athletic with massive, brawny shoulders. On his knees lay the remains of a cigarette. From time to time, his face twitched—he was caught in the middle of the gearbox of existence. But immediately next to the window, a girl, a young woman, was sitting. Her hair was blonde and unbound and cascading onto her supple shoulders like a fragment of a mighty river. She had glanced at me upon my entrance into the compartment. Now she was laying out the individual segments of an orange in a row on a page from a newspaper. She coated each piece of fruit in sugar and then popped them, one after another, into her ruby-hued mouth. All the while she was apparently listening to the monotonous onslaught of the wheels, to the sound of the rails as they flowed past.

She was still very young. The part of the luggage rack above her head was chock-full of boxes and suitcases. I hid my face in my coat so that I could undisturbedly rest my gaze on this feminine form. Her supple hands plucked at her dress, pulled something out from under the newspaper page, shoved another piece of fruit into her mouth, passed across the steamed-up windowpane and finally came to rest on her beautifully developed bosom for a fairly long interval.

Suddenly the young woman looked up. She leaned over and shook a person whom I had so far not noticed and who had fallen asleep at the opposite corner of the window.

'August,' the young woman said; she repeated the name a couple of times and then smiled.

'What is it, my child?'

'Father, you've got to eat now,' said the young woman.

'Yes—' the oldish man rejoined.

'Really, it's been ages since we left the station. You've got to eat something, August—'

Suddenly there was some movement in the invisible corner. The young woman unwrapped sandwiches, shoved the orange-segments into the middle of the tabletop, placed an apple beside them and said, 'August, please eat!'

The oldish man bent forward. He was grey at the temples; he had a nose like the beak of a prehistoric bird; his hands darted upwards like talons, snatched at a piece of fruit and then sank. This action was repeated a few times, until the young woman said, 'We've come a good long way already.'

For a moment all was calm.

'Where are we?' asked the oldish man.

'Past Munich,' said the young woman.

'Past Munich . . .'

The two of them listened to the roaring din of the train.

'It's going to rain tomorrow,' said the young woman. She bent forward to adjust something on her father's coat.

'A good child,' he sighed.

'I'm so glad we managed to catch the train,' she said. 'We might just as easily have failed to catch it. We must gain time. The train stations are ice cold at night now. This way we're safe. Do you remember the girl at the station in Vienna?'

'Yes—'

'I'd somehow seen her before somewhere.'

'Do you think so?'

'Definitely, August!'

The oldish man consumed an apple.

'I always see myself in children like that,' she said. 'Everything is in them. I don't know how to put it, but everything is contained in them. Do you know that, Father?'

The young woman consumed some of the orange segments.

'You should eat your fill,' she stated. 'You need to. This isn't going to be easy. Once we're up there, in Bremerhaven, we'll already have accomplished quite a lot. I'm very glad we're here, and yet I'd rather travel by day. One can't see anything. A few lights—one can't see anything but lights. They'll be waiting for us up there…'

'It's better to travel at night,' said the oldish man. 'Everything is easier to take. You should sleep, my child, you're tired.'

'I'm not tired. I am never tired when we're travelling. You know full well that when we took that trip to Italy, I wasn't tired either. I can never sleep on the train. On the train, I always prefer talking—and eating,' she laughed.

'Think away the hours and sleep,' her father said. 'Sleeping through a couple of hundred kilometres is a very good use of time, my child. Sleeping, dreaming, being elsewhere . . . Get some shut-eye before we get to Bremerhaven . . .'

The young woman closed her eyes.

'How quickly everything's happening,' she said. 'A year ago, we didn't know anything at all yet. I only met Eduard a year ago. You went into the hospital . . . But you look good now. You haven't looked so good in such a long time . . . A man like you, August, who should be able to show something . . .'

'Yes,' the oldish man calmly said.

'The doctor said you would outlast everybody. They have good hospitals over there, good doctors. Eduard will start earning money right away. I will too—and as for you and mother, the two of you will get some rest. There's no chance at all of anything going awry. The factories over there pay really well. Hasn't Eduard signed the contract? Everything's set down in writing in it. We can set up everything for ourselves, it says . . . Won't you have something to drink, August?'

'Sure,' he said.

The young woman handed him the thermos.

'Good,' he said, 'this will warm me up.'

Softly the young woman said, 'When we get to Bremerhaven, we'll drink something hot right away . . .'

'You are so good, Herta,' whispered the oldish man. He leaned far back.

'Eduard has already received a week's advance pay. And of course we're bound to find a place to live right away. After all, we've got a good contract. It's a sure thing all around. And Montreal is a lovely city. Eduard's got pictures of it. Can you imagine it—everybody's got their own car. We'll soon have our own car too . . .'

'Yes,' said her father.

'Here we couldn't even have gotten an apartment. And even if we had, we wouldn't have managed to get a car . . . Do you hear me, August?'

Her father said, 'Yes, I hear you, my child.'

Meanwhile, my gaze had alighted on the others. The fat woman across from me had shifted her position several times, but her newspaper had still not fallen to the floor. The young athlete remained quiescent. On his left wrist gleamed two watches. His white cuffs were an essential element of his affluence and starkly contrasted with the numerous pieces of shabby luggage belonging to the young woman who, with her father, with her whole family, was travelling to Canada . . . As we passed through a fairly large station, the compartment was violently shaken—but the sleepers did not wake up.

'They'll be delighted when you get there,' said the young woman. 'Eduard hasn't seen you in a long time. I'm glad I picked you up from the hospital myself. Had you been expecting me?'

'Yes,' said the oldish man.

'I can't believe we're going to Canada . . .'

The oldish man said nothing further.

'Had you ever given any thought to the fact that we were going to be emigrating?'

'No, never.'

'It must be quite far away, Canada—'

'It is far away, my child.'

'I won't get seasick. On a big ship one doesn't get seasick.* It really won't be many more days at all—and then we'll be in Canada . . .'

The young girl's eyes were shining.

'You should finish off the food,' she said, 'we have plenty more in the bag.'

Her father reached for one of the sandwiches.

'They're from our baker's, August. Funny, isn't it? We really ought to take the paper bag with us as well. I've brought along lots of things that will remind me of Vienna . . .'

She arranged her hair.

'In Canada, I'll need new dresses,' she stated. 'But the ladies' suits over there won't be unfashionable either. They have such lovely, colourful fabrics . . .'

'You're in rare form,' said her father.

The young woman pushed the orange segments over to him.

'You should eat some fruit,' she said. 'The doctor told me that nothing but fruit could make you totally healthy. Everybody who has trouble with their lungs should eat fruit and consume lots of fat.'

The train accelerated.

The man's hands came into view.

'Eat as many of them as you like,' she said.

---

* See Mrs Kant in *Immanuel Kant*: 'My husband isn't seasick / He's never seasick.' (*Save Yourself if You Can*, p. 240) [Trans.]

He nodded.

By now I was dead tired: I had boarded a long-distance train that was covering hundreds of kilometres without stopping. My bones ached no matter how often I shifted my position in my seat.

'Canada must be a grand country,' said the young woman. 'I'll manage to love it.'

'Perhaps, my child—'

'Vienna is already a long way behind us. Maybe we'll go back there someday. When we're rich, we'll take a trip back there. Then we'll visit the poorhouse and hand out nice things . . .'

The oldish man heaved a deep sigh.

'Vienna has also changed,' he said.

'I'm actually nervous about being on that great body of water. Don't ships still sink nowadays?'* The young woman had to keep talking. 'But it's safer than taking a plane. Mother will be astonished, she's never even been to the seashore in her life. The ocean is a huge thing to experience, isn't it, August? It's vast. We'll deal with it. We've already dealt with

---

* (1) 'Sink' in the original is a form of *untergehen*. See 'The Decline of the West' (p. 53, footnote). (2) See Kant's anxieties about the fate of the ship on which he is crossing the Atlantic in *Immanuel Kant*: 'Just think of the Titanic [. . .] All those people / with their luxury / who went down with the ship / The dance band played while the whole ship was going under [. . .] (To STEWARD) Aren't you are ever afraid / of going down with the ship / Are you a swimmer . . . He's a non-swimmer / In your place I'd be worried / night and day' (*Save Yourself If You Can*, p. 215). [Trans.]

so many things here . . . Today nothing is impossible any more, is it, Father? Over there, on the far side of the ocean, is a better life . . . Father!' The young girl leapt to her feet. 'You're terribly pale,' she said.

The others didn't believe it, but I knew that the oldish man was dead. By now I have seen lots of people die. The oldish man had died peacefully. The others couldn't comprehend it at all, but I thought that there was even such a thing as a beautiful death.

At the next station, he was carried out of the train. Everything takes its course. I assisted the young woman, helped her carry her boxes and suitcases out onto the station platform. She was now at a loss what to do next—but some people came up and took care of everything for her. The station was deserted and quite a long way from Bremerhaven. A couple of drunks could be heard howling in the refreshment room. Pieces of paper drifted across the asphalt . . .

By the time the train was in motion again, the new day was already dawning. The oldish man vanished in the darkness, and for some time afterwards I could still hear the young woman sobbing.

'August,' she kept saying; 'August, this simply can't have happened . . .'

Human beings are alone.

I had taken the dead man's seat. The uneaten orange segments had been left on the tabletop. The fat woman and the athlete had vacated the compartment. I was on my own.

The next morning, I was standing on a piece of Altona. It was made of rock. And then, later, I beheld Hamburg, the city, the harbour, and the sea, unfathomable and infinite behind the layer of fog—and somewhere out there, I thought, must lie Canada: the land of lumberjacks, canned-food factories and a better life . . .*

---

* *Altona*: a borough of Hamburg. *Lumberjacks*: In the original this is *Holzfäller*, which may also be translated as 'woodcutters'. *Holzfäller* figure prominently throughout Bernhard's work, and the verb *holzfällen*, meaning to fell trees, furnishes the title and central motif of his 1984 novel that is known in English as both *Cutting Timber* and *Woodcutters*. [Trans.]

The Story of a Man Who Left Home to See the World

From his grandfather, Gaun had inherited a roving spirit, a savage vagrancy of the soul. This old man, who had eventually suffocated in agony and was dissolving in wisdom, had done a good deal of rambling in his time. As a youngster, he had left behind the family's wood-frame house, had gone out into the world like many of his kind at the turn of the century, had seen Germany and France, had disembarked at the island of Lokrum, had eaten fish in Katoro and had watched a couple of bullfights in Spain. He didn't come back until the thirties. Back then, his sister was still alive; she kept the house tidy and managed her own businesses. She traded in flour and butter. On Sundays, her little white apron would flutter through the verdure of her garden; her spectral laughter would suffuse its paths, and when her brother came home from his military expedition through the tumbledown mess

---

Originally published as 'Von einem, der auszog die Welt zu sehen' in the Vienna-based journal *Morgen. Monatsschrift freier Akademiker* in March 1956. [Trans. after Bernhard's editors]

that was the world, in which he learnt to hunger and thirst in every direction, she threw her arms around his neck and cried, 'So he's come back after all, the old scallywag!* Have you written down everything you've seen?'

From that day on he led a sedentary existence. He wrote about his experiences in thick ledgers and took long walks. He would sit down in the hunter's tower past the last houses on the very outskirts of town, towards the peat bog, and there, as he put it to himself, he let Paris and Le Havre, London, and Copenhagen, the great cities of the world, their light-shafts of humankind's dead-history, come to life and assume colossal dimensions before his big, aged eyes; he beheld the double-decker buses of the British metropolis, the spires of Paris, the broad sinuous sweep of the Thames and the melancholy scintillation of the Seine. On that day, at the hour when he realized that he would never again manage to travel beyond the white mountains, he started growing old. He sat and sat; when it was summer, he sat in the hunting tower, and in the winter he sat in the downstairs parlour before the fire, his legs swathed in a coarse wool blanket. As the red and blue flames crept into the empty spaces of night, and Anna, his wife, brewed coffee, the old man would think back on his wanderings, on the bundle he had carried on his back all his life, on the trades he had plied between Vienna and the westernmost tip of Ireland.

---

* In the original text this is *Gauner*, hence an untranslatable pun on *Gaun*. [Trans.]

On long evenings, Gaun would loll in the parlour, and his grandfather would tell him stories. It was like being in the company of the great poets; one could have written down every word as it fell from his lips; his utterances could have been turned into noble books, books full of adventure, full of wisdom and sympathy with the hungry mouth of humankind.

'Son,' said the old man to his grandson, 'take off! Go out of here and forget where you came from! Immerse yourself in the crowds of people. Roam among the legs of your fellow citizens like a stray dog and try to make yourself an experience out of that massive agglomeration!'

His grandson opened wide his mouth and eyes and tried to make sense of the old man's words. He was talking about the cities of light, about the great double smokestacks of ocean liners.

'A person who stays at home and feeds on nothing but milk and butter is a person who has gone to seed. You've got to get a look at the world if you want to annihilate, just as you've got to get a look at it if you want to celebrate.'

These words seemed to be emanating from the very fires of hell.

'What's really worrying me,' said the old man, who was sitting in his armchair, 'is my uncertainty as to whether you'll ever get a hankering to see Pompeii, the sunken city. Have you ever had a hankering to see Pompeii?'

And his grandson asked: 'Where is Pompeii?' And his eyes blazed and stood out against the nocturnal background like those of a cat, and the old man shifted his position in the armchair and spread his fingers across his crown of white hair.

'Pompeii is the summit of the ancient world!'

Then he leaned back, and he looked as though he were sleeping, as though by some miracle he were sleeping high above the warm earth. He repeated the monumental name 'Pompeii' a couple of times; then his grandson sensed his chest tightening and his heart beginning to yearn exultantly for Pompeii, for the summit of the ancient world.

From that day on, Gaun was forever standing at the highest point in the neighbourhood and gazing down at the town below. A person must gaze down at the world to be capable of becoming a human being in the fullest sense. The disorderly jumble of rooftops, the spires, the smoke that was ascending from the red and grey chimneys, the train that was puffing out blue gases into the afternoon air, the gardens and the smokestacks of the distant cellulose factory; all this had been sucked dry, and every human being, every animal and tree, every flower and the sky itself had long since taken shape in the young man.

'I will tell anybody who shies away from going to the very corners of the earth that he is bound for ruin.* He is damned. It is not beauty alone that has been created to fill out the edifice that surrounds us. There are also the pools, the turbid waters that have been provided for us to plunge into, provided to encourage us to seek out everything—the humble sitting

---

* *Ruin*: in the original, this is the significant Bernhardian word *Untergang*. (See 'The Decline of the West', p. 53, footnote) [Trans.]

rooms of poor people, tenement houses, each and every morning and each and every evening, bridges and rivers, the currents, the cataracts that hurl us into a different life!'

Old Gaun had set out on his wanderings with a single pair of shoes and a dirty coat and a pair of trousers with pockets that had been made to last a decade. There was not a single obstacle that he failed to surmount. He led an animalistic existence and thereby ended up living just like the wild old horses at the forests' edges in the heart of England, and feeding on birds and grass, on fish and berries. He also read a great many books and fashioned himself a firm personal philosophy. 'He knows everything!' the people in the neighbourhood said after his homecoming. They stood in awe of the electricity of his bare brain.

And now, in the shade of the expiring day, the old man said: 'Nobody can take what you know away from you! Knowledge is power—an old saying: whoever knows nothing is a nincompoop. And it'll always be thus! You must do something for your mind. It is not enough to lie in the grass, to keep your eyes open, to hearken to the music of the brook, to sing of cattle and proud billy goats. A human being must listen attentively and read and keep moving. He must behold at least one new landscape each day. If he fails to behold anything, he will go to seed. A human being goes to seed quickly. Just take a look at the old asses that used to sit next to me in the schoolroom. What did they ever amount to?'

Then he turned proud and sat bolt upright: 'One man spends his entire life as a butcher! Another spends his entire life building houses! All his life he tastes lime, mortar, the nakedness of humankind! For forty years, they stand behind a counter and pour sugar into little blue paper bags, to say absolutely nothing of those who are dead and have long since forfeited their graves because nobody is paying the rent on them anymore. Or do you want to end up like the crazy beat cop who sits in the poorhouse and slurps up soup, nothing but soup, every day, and who has his very bedsheet snatched away from under his bare bottom? No, that is the wrong world! That is the rationality of the irrational! A human being lives only once, as briefly as nothing. His life melts on his tongue before he has even tasted it. If it were up to me, privation, some kind of bitter privation, would force you to leave, naked and green as you are, to leave this safe little spot. You'll be better off owning nothing but your brain and taking off and rolling along the highways like a filthy dumb animal, spat on in disgust wherever you go, than owning a shop and perching face to face with your buddy the beer mug into your seventieth year! That town down there went to seed long ago. Damn it, I tell you, I still remember the girls who used to put on a pastoral play in the parish priest's rose garden. Where are those girls now? Where are they? Having grown old, they have breasts. Having grown insatiable, they have fleshy faces that exude the ravenous greed of starved lions. Ah, if only they were like the lions! But they have nothing any longer! They feed their children—which is not to be sneezed at, Gaun!—they stand at their stoves so they can play at being mothers, and from New Year's Day until Christmas Eve they think of nothing but soup and tenderized beef.'

And all this was quite true; this old man was no man at all in the way that Gaun's male acquaintances were. The doctor would invite him over to his house to learn new things about the world from him. He, Gaun's grandfather, was the only person in town who had the English newspaper and the *Cultural Supplement* delivered to his house.

'Culture is the most important thing,' he said, 'everything else is boring. But perhaps you take an interest in cattle futures? I assuredly don't! If you're interested in culture, you can definitely count on becoming a happy human being. Hogs don't make people happy. Happiness comes, rather, from the verses of the poets—Shakespeare and Goethe and Hofmannsthal. And Emerson and good old Walt Whitman also number among them.'

Now, at this moment, he was immortal, as he grabbed his pipe, tamped down the tobacco with his thumb, and then, like a martyr, a regal martyr, gazed out the window of his wooden castle.

And so they lived, these fortunate souls who no longer had a house, or a rock, or a leaf to call their own, but merely a yearning for these things—for a house, a stone, a leaf in the wind.

The Pig-Keeper

> This dog belongs to me, said those wretched children, that spot there is my place in the sun . . .
>
> *Pascal**

Every human being gets old. Korn can sense this. At night, he dreams of endless forests and colossal cities. But they are all sited so far behind him that he can no longer summon up the courage to enter them. He lies awake for hours and waits for the next train to materialize over in the gorge.

Sweat runs down his back, his heart pounds, his hands clench and he bites the bedspread. But the disaster is never long in coming. The train must follow the track, and on each occasion, once it has reached the walnut tree, the floor sags and the entire house trembles and threatens to collapse onto Korn's bed. From time to time, he gets sick of being in bed,

---

Originally published as 'Der Schweinehüter' in the 1956 installment of *Stimmen der Gegenwart*. [Trans. after Bernhard's editors]

* *Pensées*, VI.53 (1871 Hachette edition). Bernhard quotes the passage in German translation. Pascal also furnishes the epigraphs of *Verstörung* and the 1980 play *Am Ziel* [The Goal Attained]. [Trans.]

and he has to get up and look out the window. At such moments, he braces himself firmly against the wall and stares at the yellow eyes as they materialize in the darkness. He has never before been so filled with hate as at the present time. He has suddenly started hating everything, every person, every train, every scrap of earth. He curses the earth because he knows that it will pitilessly devour him. Mercy is not mercy by any means. If only he never had to wake up in the morning ever again, he thinks. Everything is pointless.

In the morning, he goes out and sticks his hand into the crack in the wall. It keeps getting bigger and bigger. Every train enlarges the crack, and so does every frost. 'Almighty God in heaven!' he shouts.

He puts on his coat and climbs into the pigsty. Not a day passes without his staring at the pig, speaking with the pig, cajoling the pig to make it fat. How beautiful such a pig can be. What wonderful eyes are embedded in its flesh.

'You haven't got anything like a heart, have you?' Korn says under his breath.

He thumps the pig on its back with a hazelnut stick and suddenly laughs out loud. The pig takes a leap at the wall and knocks its head against it. The pig grunts with delight, with love of life, and pokes its snout around in the vegetable soup which has been standing in the sun for three days. A horrible stench rises from the soup, but Korn cannot smell it.

He bursts out laughing and addresses his pig as his 'darling'.

'You, my darling, are my only salvation—you, a pig!' he says. He leans against the wooden plank and peers into the pen. He reflects on how wonderfully the back of a pig shines, on what a magnificent shade of pink is surging up in its floppy ears, almost like a new day's sun.

'It's alive,' he whispers.

The pig grunts, lifts its snout and stares at him. Its moist muzzle trembles and quivers. Korn would like nothing more than to leap over the wooden plank and romp about on the floor with the pig.

But Korn remains standing on the other side of the plank. It is as if he is nailed to the spot. His eyes bore into the pig fat, and his mouth twists into a smile, for he knows that this pig, when it is slaughtered on Good Friday, will weigh more than a hundred and forty kilograms! Then he will drive into town with the meat and sell it at the market. Even after he has sold everything, a good fifty kilograms of pure bacon will still be left over. The bacon will be cured and hung in halves in the chimney. Then at Christmastime he will be a happy man, because he will buy a couple of bags of pears and make cider out of them, and Marie will bake white bread and sing songs to the accompaniment of her guitar.

'If there were any point to it,' Korn says to his pig, 'I would stuff those rotten onions from the cellar into your maw now as well. But there's no point anymore. Fattening time is over. I could even cut you to pieces today, but I'm not about to do that. I'm not about to soil myself with your blood today. Is your blood sweet? The sole purpose of pig's blood is to be seasoned with pepper and to taste good.'

Korn lectures the pig until it lays its head down on a pile of dirty straw and starts to snore. But Korn cannot deal with a snoring pig. He thinks about his sleepless nights, about the thoughts that torment him, about God who keeps leaving him in the lurch when he really needs him. The pig greedily bores ever deeper into its slumber. He suddenly loathes it because he loves it. He cannot hear its grunts strengthening and lengthening; he can no longer see the brute's scrawny tail bobbing up and down. He feels a strong urge to jump over the plank and trample the pig underfoot, to trample it until it squeals out its death cry and perishes. An execrable urge, but he cannot contain it. He squeezes the stick between his fingers, lifts it into the air and glances at the wall glistening with grease. Now he can smell the pig. He hardly dares to breathe. All is silent. His muscles tensed, he expectantly abides the grunting sound of the pig, abides it until the pig's tail is curved downwards and its left eye is twitching. Then he bursts out laughing, leaps up and screams as he strikes a blow on the unsuspecting pig's snout. With a horrifying squeal of pain, the animal is jerked into the air. It is as if the Devil were leaping out of an abyss. Korn strikes blow after blow, once across the pig's snout and from then onward on its back, until he is out of breath and his heart swiftly skips a couple of beats. He drops the stick and clutches at his chest. Sweat runs down his pallid face. The pig is howling. It suddenly races from one end of the sty to the other, rolls around on the floor, rears up on its haunches and collapses. Blood is streaming out of its red snout.

'I've got the power of life and death over my pig,' says Korn.

The brute calms down and lays its head down in the straw.

'It's *my* property,' says Korn, 'I can do what I like with it. It's my pig! I bought it, I fattened it, I love it, I hate it, and nobody will sell it but me. That's right: nobody but me! But I don't want it to perish today, not today. It must die on Good Friday.'

As Korn uttered these words, he was peculiarly calm, and he felt as though all his words made sense.

But suddenly he is assailed by a terrible pang of anxiety; he feels cold as the pig bleeds and its fat legs twitch, and he bends down over its rough, shiny hair and runs his bare hand along its pulsating back. And his hands, which have so far been numb and cold and hard, begin to tremble, and his lips begin to quiver, and the blood in his body rears up against him.

'Why did I beat you?' asks Korn.

He kneels down in the muck; he forgets all about his boots. He slides his hand into the pig's mouth; he can feel the animal's hot tongue inside it. He picks up a clump of straw and wipes the blood off the animal's snout. Its entire fat body is vibrating the way a human being vibrates in mortal terror. Korn shudders at the sight of the animal which is trembling with pain, and he shudders even more at the thought that *he* was the one who dealt it those terrible blows.

Three times in succession he whispers to himself: 'It's a pig, and I am going to sell it . . .'

But it is no use. Those bulbous, radiant eyes are undeceivable. They gaze at the mollified man and refuse to let go of him. They follow him to the door, to the garden, out into the woods.

When he comes back an hour later, the pig is still lying on the floor, and it seems to Korn as though in the meantime its eyes have seen nothing but him leaping across the brooks, sitting down on a tree stump, knocking over the toadstools with his boots, running to and fro like a savage.

He does not say another word to the pig. He bends over it, and he is overwhelmed by disgust at his world.

'It's alive,' he moans.

Then he waits until it moves. Slowly it pulls a foreleg out of the muck, then the second one, and finally it tries to lift itself up.

Korn does not budge. He is captivated by the miracle of the renewal of life. He has never before witnessed a resurrection at such close quarters or so distinctly. And this pig is a destiny, of this there can be no doubt. No, this pig is a life like any other, but it is an inferior life, enslaved here to be weighed by the kilogram.

Three times the brute lifts itself up, and each time it collapses. It grunts, and the tremulous quality of the sound coming from the animal's quivering throat digs deep into Korn's heart. He can hardly stand to remain here any longer, but he stays put. He leans back against the dirty outer wall of the house. He can bear to see anything apart from the pig's eyes.

Never again, he says to himself.

When the pig is finally standing and digging into the straw with its snout, Korn knows that it is not going to die before Good Friday. It will not even think of trying to slip through his hands, and he shudders at the thought that this tortured life that has just climbed up out of the deepest of abysses is only going to last another two days. Two days! But the pig knows nothing, no longer sees anything. The first steps it ventures to take lead to the trough, but the trough is empty, and the pig grunts, and Korn goes downstairs into his cellar and fetches the rotten onions. He brings back an entire armful. He drops them into the bucket, fills the bucket with water at the well, throws in some old potatoes and stirs. As he is doing so, it occurs to him to add a couple of withered cabbage leaves. So he goes and fetches them from the garden. He rolls up his sleeves and mashes the contents of the bucket into a pulp. From time to time, he averts his face from the stupefying stench of the onions. But he knows why he has taken on this job. If there's a good-sized crowd at the market, thinks Korn, and luck is more or less on my side, I'll be a rich man in just a couple of days. And there's nothing people here like more than pork. I'll sell everything myself. I'll put on a white apron and set up a stall. And when they see what fine pork I'm selling, they'll all come to see me. They'll be fighting to get to the front of the queue! Then I'll be able to buy new boots and get Marie a couple of dresses. I'll have the well pipe fixed and pay for some shingles for the roof.

I mustn't have anything hanging over my head!

He is sweating even more than earlier. But his heart has calmed back down. He picks up the bucket and takes it into the sty. The pig smells the food and rushes up to him.

'Watch your step now!' says Korn.

He shakes the pulp into the trough in such a way that little flecks of it splash back on to his face. Overwhelmed by disgust, he turns away. Then he puts down the bucket, wipes his forehead and listens to the pig slurping away.

At midday, he sits down at the table and spoons up the soup from the bowl that Marie has put there for him. He is hardly hungry, because he thinks too much, and a thinking person fancies that his belly is pretty much full at every time of day. To be sure, if she had roasted some pork instead, he would be eating with much more gusto. But this stuff? As he raises the spoon to his lips, he thinks about his pig, and he says to Marie who is sitting across from him with undone hair and lovely eyes: 'Have you ever taken a good look at that sow?'

'No,' says Marie.

'Take a real good look at her sometime!'

'Whatever for?'

Korn loses his temper.

'Don't ask such stupid questions,' he says irately.

Marie puts down her spoon and begins rising from the table. She presses her lips together and makes as if to leave.

'Keep your seat,' says Korn.

But Marie draws herself up to her full height and vanishes through the doorway and into the bedroom.

Now she's going to start howling, thinks Korn.

He wanted to ask her if she had ever had similar thoughts on looking at the pig, thoughts that make you forget where you came from and where you are going. But that is all pointless. You can't discuss things with women: he looks around the kitchen, and everything seems old and dirty to him. And as he is thinking about Marie, about how she was once young and beautiful and how she kissed him down in the reeds at the brook and boxed his ears, and how he bit her arm, causing her to cry out and run off a fair distance into the woods, he can hear her whimpering behind the door.

It has been a long time indeed since he last felt an emotion as harrowing as the one that is now assailing him with main force. What he would really like to do is lunge into the bedroom and forget everything, everything, to lunge in there and scream. But he silently traverses the floorboards with his fingers pressed together; the blood is coursing through his head, and stupefyingly savage currents of it are circulating in his brain, and he kicks open the door with his booted foot and sees nothing but his wife's blazing black eyes, her hands which she is fearfully holding up in front of her face; he sees her healthy body, which slowly shrinks farther and farther from him with every step he takes, until the empty bed precludes all possibility of flight, and he sees Marie sinking down onto the bedspread silently, without a trace of wistfulness, and welcoming him with wide-open eyes.

As he comes to from his frenzy, he realizes that his fingers are encircling her wrists, and he stands up and leaves her there like a fleshly body with its miraculous face in which all the sadness and all the beauty and the totality of wretchedness on earth are buried. He suddenly perceives an aversion to his existence and feels like using one of his hard thoughts to tear asunder the stone walls that surround him; he feels like running far away, out into the countryside, where he can gaze upon the world with an unfurrowed face, without being overwhelmed by his terrible disgust even once. He would now have given anything for an instant of genuine beauty, for a handful of piety. Smiling, but begrimed to his very depths, he goes to the door, and he thinks of what curious paths are travelled by mankind, of the puddles that they are obliged to wade through, while outside the sun is shining and the surface of the lake is holding its peace and a couple of birds are singing somewhere on the boughs of the forest.

'And then you always leave me here on my own, always drop me,' says Marie, and she can feel the veils and illusions falling away from her and she parts her lips, and it seems as if she is thinking about how she could get her husband back.

'Dreadful, it's all dreadful,' she says, and wracked by bitter agony, she turns towards the other side of the room and begins to loathe her husband who picks up his coat and leaves the house.

He walks diagonally across the field; his boots sink deep into the mud. He cuts a branch from a willow shrub to use as a walking stick and crosses the bridge spanning the brook. He stops beside the tall, old, furrowed oak tree and stares into the dark water in which the willows are reflected like ghosts. There is not a human soul in sight. The farmers are all at home, playing cards or sweatily cutting open the bellies of pigs so that they will be ready for Easter Sunday and be able to abandon themselves to gluttony, to the cider and the doughnuts that cracklingly crumble between their teeth. But he is no farmer. He will not be eating any doughnuts on Easter Sunday because Marie does not know how to bake them. She only knows how to bake white bread and to roast pork. He cheerfully thinks about how much he is looking forward to the pork roast, and then gazes into the oily water-filled ruts left by the vehicles that have passed through here since the most recent rainfall.

It is April, but Korn sits down in the grass which is barely a finger high, and digs his boots into the moist, loamy earth. Once upon a time he was a child here in this neighbourhood, then a boy, then a lad who wrung pheasants' necks, and one fine day he had woken up and they had regarded him as a proper man. And he knows exactly when he turned into a proper man. That was on that evening when he had been on his way home from a wedding. It was over there behind the hay barn. But the barn is now abandoned, and there is nobody, no matter how long he were to stand there, who will ever be capable of totally and completely fathoming that moment that signifies the beginning of a new life for him. A new life! Korn can no longer bear to look over at the wooden hut. The new lives are terribly old, he thinks. The new lives have been annihilated!

He has started feeling warm, and when he presses his palms into the half-naked earth, he senses the approach of summer. What will this summer bring him? What has this summer got in store for him? The beautiful summers are over, thinks Korn. There used to be beautiful summers. He used to have nights in which he would sleep till dawn and listen to the crickets chirp. And he used to have dreams beyond anybody's power of invention! Back then, he would lie in bed with his arms and feet stretched out and gaze into the nights, which were so beautiful that he could not help feeling ashamed of himself even much later. When he gazes at the mountains in the distance, he knows very well that they are no longer the same mountains that he saw ten and twenty years ago. The trees are also different. The grass is different. The people are different; they live in the houses over there and get drunk every day and consequently bring into the world children who only grow up to be a metre-and-a-half tall. Indeed, and then they go dancing and slip into the haystacks, and when they come out it is all over. Nobody knows what he is letting himself in for when he crawls into the haystacks. He himself crawled into them as well. Now he cannot get the thought of this out of his head.

'Every brute crawls into them,' he says.

He wipes the sweat off his face.

They go to church in exactly the same way they crawl into the haystacks. Their prayers are always the same. And they are also my prayers.

Suddenly the sunbeam has wandered off and Korn feels cold. He leaps to his feet and begins running. When he is sure that nobody can see him, he shakes his entire body in a completely haphazard manner; at that moment he is a hodge-podge of thousands of emotions and walks like a king one minute and a beggar the next. And he bursts into bestial laughter and thumps his walking stick against his boots.

He does not know how long he has been wandering around in the woods. But by the time it starts getting dark, he is already heading back. And as he hears the clock in the village striking the hour, he suddenly feels hungry again, and this hunger gnaws at him like an incurable illness. If anybody has never forsaken him in his life, hunger and thirst have not. The older he gets, the more he needs in order to keep going. In the old days, it was enough to take some bread and cider and fresh air in the evening. But later, after he left the area and went roaming through the cities and the swamps, when he started romping about with girls and having to grapple with loutish blokes on building sites, bread was no longer enough. Then he needed beer and bacon and pork in copious amounts. He drank milk by the litre, and all of a sudden he came to abhor apples which he had loved so much in his youth, and he no longer took any pleasure in their smell or in their sour sweetness as it trickled into the corners of his mouth when he bit into them. This machine that he had built for himself over time had to be maintained singlehandedly by him. But he never shunned a job! He did everything that a human being who wants to live can do; he ploughed, sweated and reaped, and he not only got to know the fields, and the barns in which the stench of the dried dung makes it impossible to breathe in the July sun, but also savoured the sewers in the cities, the lacerated streets in which sweat matters more than anywhere else. Until they half shattered his skull in the war and bestowed a pension on him, he had always been hungrily hitchhiking through the world. Then with his own hands, along with Marie's, he built himself the house and went to bed and stayed there for three whole weeks. And right after the end of the first spring, he noticed the first crack in the wall, and from then on out he had not enjoyed a single restful hour.

'Not a single one,' says Korn under his breath, and thoughts like this begin to worm into him, as they worm into so many people, and he tries to keep his mind fixed on thinking up a way of getting out of the horrible situation in which he now finds himself. He locks his hands together behind his back and walks along the railway embankment. As his footfalls become more and more calmly measured, the thumping of his heart becomes more and more agitated. But however intently he thinks, all the paths he surveys terminate at some obscure cranny of the world, at some site of pure night and darkness. There is no mercy!

'I have failed,' Korn whispers.

A couple of metres shy of his house he stops walking. The windows of his sitting room are brightly lit. If he were another person, he would go in there and be happy. But he is his same old self. He will never be able to slip out of his skin.

In the grass, the crickets are chirping. Nobody understands the magnitude of the fear that is making him tremble. Nobody, however close to him he may be, understands a single thing about this solitary human being whose ear is perpetually turned to the gorge from which trains materialize. He has closed his eyes and is waiting. But no train appears, and the night is cold, and with rapid footfalls the man heads for his house. He opens the door of the pigsty and peers in. The moon is shining on the pig. The pig grunts. It is alive! Korn is content. He turns around and inhales deep draughts of the evening air.

His wife appears in the front doorway. She is wearing her clogs, and over her dress, a coarsely woven apron.

'Come in,' says Marie.

She stretches her hands out towards him and pulls him into the house.

'I'm not tired any more,' she says and fetches beer and cider and puts a slice of bacon on the table.

He eats and thinks about his pig. He pictures it getting bigger and fatter.

'I'm thinking about how I'm going to sell the pig,' he says. They do not speak to each other beyond this point. They rise from the table and go to bed. They behold the night and are filled with loathing.

As Marie is sleeping uninterruptedly on her side, he thinks that his life is over. I must put an end to it, he thinks. I must smash it to pieces; there's no point to it any more!

The man cannot sleep. He turns around and looks into Marie's face. But the young woman is sleeping soundly and her long breaths are calm. Korn loves her, but now he loathes the very breath in her breast. He gazes at her forehead, which the moon is illuminating as it traverses the fields outside; at her eyelashes, which lie above her soft, well-proportioned cheeks. He shoves the bedspread off his chest and sits up. He gets out of bed gently. But the floorboards creak when the tips of his toes touch them. He feels chilly. He takes a couple of steps to the trunk chest and pulls out his coat. Then he looks into Marie's face once again, worrying that she might have observed him, and opens the door. He goes outside and inhales the air which here, near the lake, is cool and biting. He can smell the water plants and the stars and the dead fish.

Korn is fearful in the darkness. He is frightened by the silent cry of a cricket, by the sobbing of a wagtail, by the flight of a bat; he is startled by the cracking of a rotten branch that was torn off the apple tree by the most recent gust of wind.

As he gazes out at the surface of the lake, his youth materializes from out of the clouds, and he thinks back on the boating trips he took with the old fisherman who used to catch enormous fish in his nets at midnight and would start praying out in the old rowboat whenever he had caught enough by his own standards. Then the strange man would kneel down, place the big fish on the wooden plank in front of him and start praising God and extolling the earth and all of heaven. Then he would murmur some strange words about birth and death, about bread and children, and with his chapped lips he would softly sing a song that followed Korn into his dreams. He sang:

'Alas poor fish.
Reddish cream;
from Fishy's mouth
peers a dream.
Don't break it up,
stay alone.
Drink the moon's
gold on your own.'

Korn hums the song, but even while its words are still on his lips, all past life strikes him as dilapidated and shattered. He thinks that people must incessantly shatter all the beautiful things in the world. They ruin everything—the songs, the cathedrals, the endless fields, the pure images of childhood.

He walks barefoot in the garden, in which he turned the first spadeful of earth the evening before. He kneels and palpates the soil with his hot fingers. It is moist and soft. It is crushable. It is still unseeded, but soon everything will be green again, and the little plants will come into bloom, and the stalks will rise and bear fruit. No, thinks Korn, this year not a single piece of fruit will grow, not a single flower will bloom here. The garden will be bare, fallow and bare.

Then he looks up at the sky, and for the span of a few breaths he sucks the air out of the darkness as he did in his childhood.

He would now be glad to be in the company of people who would destroy this scene for him. But they do not live out here. They live where the trains end up. And Korn's eyes fix on the track and follow the silver trail that ends over there by the elder bushes. The railway is his destiny and his nemesis. He takes a couple of steps towards the house to take a look at the big crack. By a year from now, it will have all come tumbling down, he thinks. He looks up at the roof timbers which are shifting, steadily shifting, like the windows which are slowly breaking to pieces and which make eerie cracking noises at midnight. The ground is cursed. He has the worst soil in the country. Never before in his life has he been so badly duped. He bought the property in the expectation of spending the rest of his life here, because he thought that everybody had to have a spot that belonged to him, a place that he could crawl away into and do whatever he liked in afterwards.

He cannot allow himself to think about the mortar, about the trunk chest, about Marie, about how she bawled at him and about how she plunged into the lime pit and he fished her out of it like a burning corpse. He has bled with incessant drudgery; he has been burned out by the sun and washed out by the rain. He pounds his fists against the outer wall of the house until his fingers are streaming with blood. He howls and collapses against the wall.

Suddenly he starts worrying that Marie might have heard him and that she is now observing him from some dark corner. He looks around, but nothing is stirring. His entire body is trembling. He stands up and sees her bed through the window. She is lying there, and she looks as though she is passing through a dream.

Exhausted, he slinks into the house. But he knows that he will be unable to sleep, takes the candle from atop the cupboard, lights it and goes back outside. Now he scrutinizes the entire house; he shines the light of the candle everywhere, into every crack, into all the joints and crevices. All the while, the moon is gazing at him, its bestial mouth agape.

He moves forward to the end of the garden and trains the light along the row of beets. A week ago, the fence was still upright. Now it has fallen over. The crumbling soil has brought it down. He says nothing and stares at the clods of earth.

In the gorge, the lights of a train materialize. The rails tremble and clink. But Korn, who has been duped out of every last vestige of a future, remains obdurate; with his eyes tightly shut, he stands firm on the soil until the roving monster propelled by colossal death's claws is gone.

His decision remains firm. He will annihilate himself. He will hang himself from a tree or bludgeon himself to death or lie down on the tracks. He will sacrifice himself to his enemy like a piece of meat. Nothing will stop him. Tomorrow, he will slaughter the pig and cut it into large pieces. He will hang the bacon in the chimney and look on as Marie tenderizes the pig's big, bulbous head, along with its eyes and brain, by boiling it in the cauldron. And he will say nice things to her and step outside as if he were going to come back soon.

When he's about to step into the house, he hears the pig. But he is now past changing his mind. He will not wait until the house collapses over his head, until he turns to begging. He will take his Good Friday morning communion, and before nightfall he will be dead. On Easter Sunday, he will be resurrected! He will choose the best means of killing himself and vanish with little or no fuss. What is a human life? he asks. What difference does one fleshly body more or less make? And the soul? Where is my soul? It torments me, it isn't worth the trouble of lugging around.

As he is stepping into the house, he realizes that he is going to hang himself from a tree, somewhere in the woods, where it will be hard to find him. He has no desire to be found right away. Ideally, he would like to rot on an undiscoverable tree, to decompose into nothing. He would like to obliterate every trace of his existence, to erase himself completely. Marie must have her pig, he thinks. I will butcher it for her so that she won't need to put herself to any trouble.

He blows out the candle, puts his coat on the lowboy and crawls into bed. Beneath the bedspread, he pictures gruesome images to himself. But the moment finally arrives when he is taken by sleep. And Korn knows nothing more of anything until Good Friday morning.

That morning is grey and its air is muggy. He immediately remembers what he was thinking before he dozed off, and he finds it wondrously spooky that his situation has not changed. It is the same as yesterday. He rises, determined to kill himself. From time to time in his youth he wanted to kill himself. Your sole salvation is death, all the objects in the room say to him. He has severed his ties with them. He no longer feels any attachment to the pictures—the dusty, old, lacerated pictures—that gawk at him from the wall. He no longer feels anything in the presence of his mother's portrait. She gazes at him with a fearsome mien from within the carved black picture frame. Her wide-open eyes detest him. He could punch himself: never before has he so palpably discerned his mother's lovelessness in this picture. The coldness of her eyes, the gloominess of her entire being. He is filled with an ever-mounting loathing of this originator of all his suffering. With a loathing of all humankind. No, he is not finding it difficult to sever his ties with the earth. It is a multimillion-faced phantom, a spectre, a madhouse. Fly from it, run as fast as you can, fling yourself out of it and into the bottomless depths. Slash you own throat, for your blood and your death are your resurrection!

He slips on his boots, washes himself and gets dressed. Then he goes and opens the drawer of the lowboy and pulls out a small cashbox. He sits down at the table and writes his will as Marie is wringing out the laundry at the window.

He bequeaths the house to Marie. He can hardly write, but what he is writing is plainly legible. He thinks about what else he is going to leave behind. He will simply bequeath everything to Marie, his wife, who loves him and loathes him and who will not give him a child. He will commit everything to her, because she also put herself through bloody hell as they were building the house and he has beaten her and she has forgiven him for it afterwards. By this point, he can scarcely keep the pen in his hand. But he pulls himself together and fills out the remainder of the sheet. He signs his name at the bottom, folds the paper, stands up, places it on top inside the cashbox and places the cashbox back in the lowboy.

For a while, he stands at the window and looks out. Marie is bending over a large basket, pulling pieces of laundry from it and then hanging them from the clothesline that stretches from the apple tree to the garden fence. Ideally, he would have said something to her, but behind the apple tree a heavy sky is spreading across the countryside as before a long rain shower. The mountains are moving closer to him and standing out clearly in the föhn air. The fields are sweating. He turns around to get everything ready for the dismemberment of the pig.

As the church bells are ringing, he sharpens the large knife. Then he washes the dust off the large iron mallet. He fetches the small knives from the kitchen and places them on the table in the vestibule. The young woman places a large bucket of water on the hot stovetop. He and Marie pull the large washtub into the middle of the tiled floor.

She is delighted, he thinks.

'It's been two years since we last slaughtered a sow,' says Marie. He says nothing in reply.

Calmly, he takes down the iron chains above the door and stretches them from the floor up to and across the washtub.

'There hasn't been one this heavy before,' says Marie, and she thinks that she will stuff the black puddings as soon as her husband has pulled out the pig's entrails.

Once they have cleared away from the vestibule everything that will not be used in the slaughtering and have all the necessary tools ready to hand, the two of them step out the front door and seat themselves on the bench.

'You'll be able to go to the market by Wednesday,' she says.

'Yes,' Korn avers, and he knows full well that Wednesday no longer means anything to him.

She wipes her fingers clean on her apron.

'On Easter Sunday I'm going to church. Whether you like it or not,' she says and gazes at the ground. 'I don't go at all the whole year.'

She is expecting her husband to lose his temper, but he simply gives her a sidelong glance and says, 'Then go!' And his brain cannot grasp how anyone can go to church when everyone knows that everything comes to naught, that he or she will be annihilated by God. Throughout her life, Marie has had a profound relationship with God. How peculiar. He loathes people who love God. This is why he wants to kill himself.

They sit next to each other silently thinking, but then Marie suddenly says in a peculiar voice, 'I am very happy.' He is acutely conscious of her hand as she takes hold of his, and just as conscious of her breath, and all at once everything inside him begins to waver, and he hears his wife speaking, and certain moments, a thousand memories, come rushing back to him; he remembers their days in the marsh and their hours of splendour in the woods, the quacking of the ducks and the water lapping against the boat, and the blue sky and the smell of the fruit trees in his garden and the stalks of grain, tall as a full-grown man, amid which as a child he used to lie down and dream long dreams, and endlessly shining nights, stars and mountaintops.

'Come on,' she says, and he feels her love, and as she races into the house, singing all the while, the entire colossal edifice that he has been raising over the past two days collapses like a lie. He sits motionless on the bench. Then he stands up and runs after his wife, and it is as if the entire ghastly world is falling off his shoulders piece by piece.

'Take care of the pig,' she says to him.

She is almost merry.

Korn goes outside to do the pig in. For the first time in a long while, he can breathe properly. It's nonsense, he thinks, nothing but nonsense. Why kill? Why annihilate oneself? Why? I am not going to kill. Not myself! I am going to take the pig to the market.

'The pig will be my salvation!' he howls with happiness.

He kicks open the pigsty and whistles a couple of notes. His burdens fall from his shoulders like a phantom. But as he is taking the cudgel down from its hook, a thrill of terror courses through his limbs. He rushes to the pen. The pig is lying motionless in the dirty straw. Its body is bloated, almost twice as fat as at its last feeding. Its legs are splayed out on all sides. On its snout glistens a large ball of yellow foam. Korn, who has flung the cudgel into the muck, leaps over the plank in a single bound and kicks the pig's carcass with his booted foot. He tramples on the pig's swollen body and like a man in the grip of demonic possession screams, 'Marie! Marie! Marie!'

The animal is awash in blood and a fetid yellow liquid is flowing from its side. In his fury, the man no longer knows what he is doing. He jerks the pig's head into the air and shakes it. He tries to turn the carcass over onto its other side, but its cold insentient flesh is heavy, and Korn stops and gazes into the muck with which the yellow juice that is still streaming out of the pig is mingling.

'Marie!' cries Korn, and at that very moment the young woman comes wheezing into the sty and starts wailing. She throws herself at the pen and stares at the brute. But for all her gazing at it, it is no longer alive; its eyelids fail to twitch, its tail is motionless.

She tugs on its hind legs and drags the carcass under the sty's small window. Marie shudders in disgust. She runs out of the sty, and Korn hears her continuing to shriek for some time. She throws herself onto the bed and tears the bedspread to pieces; she races in and out of the room like a savage while Korn stands in the darkened corner of the sty and never takes his eyes off the pig. He clutches at the wall and tears his nails. When he takes just one good look at the closed swollen eye of the sow, from which the fetid juice is flowing, his stomach heaves and he bends over into the corner. He wipes his mouth clean with his arm, and now shivering with the sudden onset of a fever, he climbs over the plank.

Later, still wearing his boots, he kicks over the table in the vestibule on which the knives are lying. He also flings the large bucket off the stove, and the boiling hot water floods every corner of the kitchen. He drags the washtub out of the hallway, lifts it high above his shoulders and hurls it over the embankment, at the bottom of which it then lies smashed to pieces. Marie stands at the bedroom window with her fists pressed against her pallid face and spectates on the handiwork of annihilation.

By now, this man on the rampage is inappeasable. She is terribly afraid that he may have completely lost his senses and that he will now not even shrink from attacking her.

He calls out her name. As if against her will, she gropes her way towards him and does what he orders her to do. She follows him into the pigsty and leans against the damp, filthy wall as Korn smashes the pen to pieces with the large iron mallet.

Later he says: 'Make yourself useful!' and she pulls the pig out of the sty and, sweating all the while, drags it along the garden fence through the wet earth. Marie collapses. Then she lifts herself back up. They lay the pig down not far from the walnut tree. They gather some twigs up into a pile. They place some rotten branches on top of the pile. Then they roll the pig up to it and cover it with bales of hay.

Feeling freezing cold, Marie sits down in the grass.

Korn walks with long strides into the house. The young woman stares at the pig that was supposed to have brought happiness and benediction. She does not know how long she has been sitting there and weeping. She cannot take this all in. It is as if hell itself in the form of their ruined house is rising before her very eyes.

When her husband walks up to her from across the lawn, she starts screaming again. But suddenly she feels ashamed in the presence of this silent person who is setting fire to the pile. The flames rise high, and a large fire devours the pig. The smoke is driven across the fields by the wind.

The two people go into the house. Korn locks himself in the bedroom. Marie sinks to her knees and prays. She looks out the window.

By dusk, only a single ember is still visible. It, too, disintegrates in the supervening darkness.

The shadows of clouds envelop the house which stands in front of the wooded area like a last sign of humanity, as the moon, holding its peace for fear of death, rises above the lake. The moon forsakes the blackened mountains and casts its beams onto the spine of the landscape. A feeble light reels out of the house and into the ditch, then moves erratically along the train tracks. It is Korn, taking flight from his abode. His footfalls increase in pace, as if the Devil were driving him across the waterlogged fields.

Korn races along like a person who dreads something. He has only one thought in his mind: to kill himself quickly. He is hauling a length of rope. He runs between the blackberry bushes, crosses the brook, pauses for a moment, wheezing, rallies his forces and dives into the woods.

In the sunken path through the woods, he trips over the roots of an enormous tree. He skins the palms of his hands and bruises his forehead. But he does not cry out. Silently, he stands back up, grabs the rope and hurries onwards. He has no specific tree in view. But it must be far enough from the house that nobody will find him for some time. He shudders as he shuddered during his first attacks of mortal terror in his childhood.

He senses the boundless beggarliness of his species.

In the middle of the woods, through which he has roamed with the animals on many a summer day, in which he has feasted on berries and mushrooms, he throws himself onto the moss and presses his face against the pliant earth. He uproots the plants, having become insensible of his body and of his blood. It was only a couple of paces. And all at once the faces of all the people he has ever encountered in his path through the world materialize before his eyes: the oedematous faces of merchants, the prostitutes with whom he spent entire weeks, the young girls, the fisherman, Marie, her mother, old men and cripples; they all pass by and stare at him. He sits up and gazes into the darkness.

They are annihilating everything, the man thinks, and he cannot get to his feet, rather, he gazes into the great event with eyes wide open. There are colossal pits that swallow up everything. The beast of midnight is gobbling up every tree, every house and farm, all the people with whom he has romped about on the threshing floor of youth, with whom he has smelled the damp odour of hay and the fumes of the pigs, with whom he has drunk the warm milk from the trembling red udders in the stables, all the people who have risen from their musty beds, all the cripples whose eyes imbibed the entire inconceivable beauty of the earth, a brother and sister who reeled past the windows depicting the Three Magi and forced their glory into their thirsty breath. Oh, when they can only swing an axe and trample on the next creature's back! But man and beast alike perish before sunrise! This is the life of the earth, says Korn, and he stands up, grabs his rope and starts looking for a tree. Now he knows that there is no longer any possibility of turning back, and the end has unfolded before him like a canopy, and the abysses are presenting themselves to him like new passages to a tranquil landscape.

He walks silently through the woods, and the smells of the moss flow into him and pervade him with pungent force. He has only a single peace in view. It lies beyond the border. It lies beyond the trains and houses, beyond all the churches and houses of God, beyond all the fraud and all rapaciousness.

Then he is at the firs, at the place where he is going to draw his final breath. He walks up to each of the trees and examines it carefully. But most of them are too weak, and Korn is worried he might hang himself on a bough that will snap off afterwards and leave him lying in agony on the ground. He wants to be sure of dying. It has to happen quickly. For that, a strong bough is necessary. But he must be able to climb it easily. Once he is up there, he will put the noose around his neck and jump. For a moment, he reflects on what an appalling sight he will be with his tongue hanging out. But he quells every emotion. He laughs so loudly that it echoes back from the depths of the woods. This echo makes him fearful anew, but he contorts his face and laughs again until he is sure that he is no longer *capable* of feeling any emotion.

At last he has found the appropriate tree. He looks around. Nobody can see him. He couldn't care less if the animals can. He slips off his boots, holds fast onto the bark of the tree and pulls himself up. Everything is happening just as he imagined it would. Now he ties the rope firmly to the bough and prepares the noose. He is strong. But as he is putting the rope around his neck, the midnight frost makes him shiver, and with eyes wide open he sees the great globe of the moon breaking forth from the blanket of clouds above the mountains. And suddenly his eyes see hot circulating blood, and as he peers into the darkness, he is startled by the most horrifying sight in his life. Between two trees he sees a large cross, to which a living human being is firmly nailed: it is Jesus Christ, the son of God, agonizingly attempting to tear his hands free of the crossbeam. Korn stares at the cross. He hears the son of God scream. Suddenly he hears a million voices, and they are all screaming around the son of God, and not a single one of them becomes visible, not a single one of them comes to help the dying man, who opens wide his gory eyes and collapses.

'Jesus! Jesus!'

Then he throws away the rope and leaps from the tree to the ground. And he runs after the crucified man, ever deeper into the night.

From all sides he hears the bells of Easter.

They are ringing, ringing, ringing!*

---

* According to his friend Wieland Schmied, Bernhard wished to end the story with Korn's suicide, but such an ending would have been unacceptable to Herold Verlag, the conservative Catholic publisher of *Stimmen der Gegenwart*. Bernhard's papers contain post-publication revisions that suggest how the original ending might have read—either with the omission of everything after the sentence corresponding to 'He slips off his boots, holds fast onto the bark of the tree, and pulls himself up,' or with the replacement of everything after the sentence corresponding to 'For a moment he reflects on what an appalling sight he will be with his tongue hanging out' with a passage that may be translated as follows: 'But only a moment. Then he kills every emotion. He rushes up the tree, sticks his head into the noose, and lets himself drop. Marie is standing at the window and waiting.' [Trans. after Bernhard's editors]

Occurrences

TWO YOUNG PEOPLE flee into a tower which formerly served as the town's citadel, and ascend it without uttering a single word. They have no wish to extinguish their silence with a betrayal, and set about their scheme with thoughtless swiftness. Halfway to the top, they glimpse an unascertainable detail of the landscape in which the tower is situated. The coldness of the walls causes them to stagger upward as if through the inside of a block of ice: with mouths agape and arms stretched forward in the hope that by means of these half-sincere gesticulations the distance they wish to cover might be artificially diminished. Now it becomes evident that the girl by force of imagination is capable of pressing forward with greater speed than the intellectually limited young man, and it is important to state that the girl, although climbing eight or ten steps behind the young man, her lover, is in truth fifteen or twenty step-lengths ahead of him. The completely

---

Written in 1959 but not originally published (as *Ereignisse* by Literarisches Colloquium Berlin) until 1969. [Trans. after Bernhard's editors]

windowless tower is a precursor of darkness and quite distinctly recognizable as such. When they finally reach the top, they undress and fall naked into each other's arms.

THE GIRL is sitting on a bench beneath an apple tree beside the front door of a castle-like building that stands in a lofty valley and that a distinguished gentleman has discovered on one of his rambles which is leading him from church to church and from one unusual architectural structure to another. He stops at the garden fence and is fascinated by the beauty of the girl who is wearing her hair in long pigtails. He acts as if he is writing something in his notebook, but in fact he is observing the girl uninterruptedly. He is being observed by the nuns who are working in the vegetable garden; but he does not notice this. He wants to avoid breaking the tension that exists between the girl and him, and so he does not even step forward to address her. But at a certain point he will introduce himself, he thinks, and strike up a conversation with the girl. He will tell her all about his travels, and lasting connections are quickly established in ways like this. He will give her an account of the world in which he lives. But at the very moment when he is making up his mind to approach the girl, the girl stretches a stockinged leg into the air and starts pulling her pigtails with both hands. Because she cannot speak, she emits incomprehensible noises. She keeps tugging at her pigtails until her eyes turn dark with blood. Only now does the man realize that he is on the grounds of a madhouse, and he leaves immediately without attracting any attention from the nuns who lay hold of the girl and drag her into the house.

THE FORTY-YEAR-OLD MAN has been catching the same bus for twelve years. As he is walking home, he reflects that somebody else is to blame for his unhappiness. That he isn't. Even though he does not know for certain who forced him into the twelve-year ordeal, he discharges a curse word at the party in question. He rounds the corner where the elder bush is shedding its leaves. Naturally, he does not see this at all. Clamped under his arm is a well-worn briefcase in which he has kept his lunch for every day of the twelve years apart from Sundays, not to mention leave days. As a rule, he does not eat any of it. It is eaten by the children when he gets home. At the spot where the road discloses to his view the house in which he lives with his family, he raises his eyes for the first time. He pictures to himself his wife setting dinner on the table and putting their children to bed. He suddenly sees his wife removing her blouse and draping it over the back of the chair. She takes a cup of coffee from the stovetop, crumbles some white bread into the cup and laps up the mixture of bread and coffee with a spoon. Now he is cold, he turns around and retraces his steps along the road. He walks through the woods and goes to bed with his mistress who owns a one-storey house with a vegetable garden. At this very instant, his wife is saying to the children: Be quiet, or else the Christ Child* won't bring you any presents.

---

* See 'A Winter's Day in the Mountains', p. 50, footnote.

THE CASHIER at an ironworks has married a woman eight or nine years his senior. Shortly after their wedding, the quarrels begin. It is with boundless antipathy to each other that the two of them fall asleep and wake up. Eventually the wife becomes gravely ill, an event that is possibly connected with her childlessness; she gets better time and again, but she suddenly loses the power of speech and can make herself understood only by using her hands; at home, she writes everything on the pages of a calendar: 'I want to go away,' for example, or 'It's lovely outside.' She hates it when people feel sorry for her. Eventually, she gets pains in her legs and grows quite stiff. She has to be pushed about in a wheelchair. She sits vigilantly at the window. When her husband gets home, he has to wheel her outside. Always along the same stretch of road. Always farther. She shakes her clenched fists at him. She is always hungrier for new houses, new trees, new people. She peers out of her weatherproof winter cape* and through the gaps between the trees on the avenue. One evening, as he is pushing her along near the edge of the road, he turns the conveyance around and tips it into the abyss. She cannot cry

* The same type of garment as the one on which Bernhard's story 'The Weatherproof Cape' centres, although here he terms it a *Winterkotzen* and there a *Wetterfleck*.

out. The metal conveyance splits into pieces. This sequence of events now resides in his dreams. But he will do something like this to her, he thinks.

THE CELLIST knows there is nothing but loathing between her and the operetta conductor. In spite of this, every day at the same hour, she slips through the door of his room and into his bed. The calamity of having turned thirty has taken possession of her and the harder she struggles against it, the more inexorably the process of her destruction advances. In the attic of the conservatory, she incessantly plays sonata movements that she plunges into for the sake of tearing them to pieces. With incredible ruthlessness she starves herself; all day long, she lies drunk in bed for the sake of subsequently pursuing her project of annihilation all the more energetically. She sells everything; she is suddenly left with nothing but a single black high-necked dress. She grips the neck of her instrument with both hands and smashes it to pieces. She steps up the pace of everything. Laughs. Is silent. After her final assignation with the conductor, she sits on a trunk full of singers' costumes in the gloomy backstage passageway and weeps.

THE BIG LANDOWNER dreams that one of his labourers is digging up the earth at numerous spots on his estate and that everywhere he digs, a corpse turns up. He has the labourer dig up the entire area around his house. But there is not a single spot under which a corpse has not been buried. Now the landowner has his entire estate dug up by hundreds of labourers, but in fact it is chock-full of corpses beneath a thin layer of soil. He has each of the turned-up corpses, which are of all ages and both sexes, shown to him, and he remembers that he has slain all these people *with his own hands*. Nevertheless, the fear of being killed himself keeps him from confessing to his crime. He alights on the idea of having *the crime or the murderer* found out. To this end, he organizes a committee of government officials whom he pays handsomely. Only a few days later, a *murderer* is discovered. Although the landowner knows that this man, who is a complete stranger, cannot possibly be the *murderer*, he has him delivered to a court of law that sentences him to death. The *murderer* is executed. In this manner, the officials discover many more *murderers*. Eventually, they discover exactly as many *murderers* as there are murder victims. They are all executed and interred on the landowner's estate. Now the landowner wakes up and gets out of bed. He goes to the woods to determine which trees he still has to have cut down this autumn. This question has been preoccupying him for days.

THE PRIEST'S SISTER falls ill one day, and when she is allowed to get back out of bed, people realize that the illness has affected her brain. She does things that a normal person under normal circumstances never does. For example, while waving a myrtle wreath, she dances across the village square, sticking out her tongue and emitting incomprehensible sounds in her progress. She is also in the habit of suddenly stepping up to the altar in the middle of mass service and strewing about rose blossoms from a little basket. Or she writes to the bishop a letter in which she apprises him that the Mother of God has said to her in the potato field that she would be happy to see the writer of the letter reside *in the church itself* from now on. Not that anybody laughs at her; people regard her anxiously, diffidently. They let her tell them stories. Among these tales there is even one to the effect that when everyone in the village without exception is asleep, the Saviour walks through the square pursued by his tormentors without saying a word and while bleeding from his stigmata. One evening, she fails to show up for supper which is taken in the parsonage's kitchen. She is searched for. Nobody can find her. First thing next morning the schoolchildren discover her frozen into the large sheet of ice behind the brewery. Her gaping mouth is larger than her face. Around her neck she is wearing, as always, a starched lace collar. Her arms are spread apart. The water froze quickly.

THE ACTOR has a part as an evil enchanter in a pantomime. He is thrust into a sheepskin and a pair of shoes that are far too small and that pinch his feet. The entire costume is so uncomfortable that he breaks into a sweat, but of course nobody notices this, and on the whole he is never happier than when acting for children, for they are the most grateful of all audiences. The children, three hundred in number, take fright when he walks onto the stage because they are entirely on the side of the young couple whom he has transformed into animals of two different species. They would ideally like to see nothing but the young couple covered from head to toe in brightly coloured clothing, nothing else, but then the play would not be a proper play, for from time immemorial a pantomime has had to include a malevolent, impenetrable figure who strives to destroy the good and the penetrable or at least make it look ridiculous. With the second rising of the curtain, the children can no longer be contained. They leap from their seats and onto the stage, and it is as if there were no longer three hundred of them but many times as many, and even though the actor is weeping underneath his mask and entreating them just to stop assaulting him with their kicks and blows, which they are administering with hard metal objects, they refuse to be swayed and keep hitting him and stomping all over him until he has ceased to move and his pale mutilated hands are jutting out into the dusty air exuded by the gridiron. When the other actors come rushing over and ascertain that their fellow cast member is dead, the children burst into a colossal collective peal of laughter that is so loud that they all lose their minds in its midst.

SEVERAL SHADOWS keep leaping out at a homeward-bound workman. They violate him on the riverbank and leave him there. The moment he tries to get up to set off on his way, the shadows are there again and strike him. They pull him out of his coat and push him into the river. They force his head under the water and pierce his eardrums with long knives. They try to hold him underwater until he asphyxiates. He recovers consciousness at a different place, and naked as he is, resumes walking. The shadows suddenly rematerialize and strangle him. They throw him into a hole; they throw him into a bomb crater and fill it in. He wakes up again and runs along the railway embankment. Now the shadows attack him without warning and fling him into the darkness. He escapes and begins running faster than before. But the shadows catch up with him. They stab him. He hears them shouting his name at the top of their voices. They fling him into the space between two blocks of stone that move towards each other and crush him to a pulp. Now he wakes up and turns on the light. He discovers his wife beside him in the bed. He puts on his coat and leaves the house for a couple of hours. In the early morning, he is seen riding his bicycle to the building site.

THE PRESIDENT has a characteristic that catches the eye of everybody who encounters him, when he is bowling and when he is drinking beer, at night and during sexual intercourse; indeed, even at the parliamentary sessions that he chairs after the advent of the great change. Hand gestures of various sorts are directed at the characteristic which nobody can explain but which is so plainly visible that it does not even elude the notice of the uninitiated. People maintain that it originated from a development that can no longer be stopped but that they wish they could stop. They recall moments at which they became aware of a phenomenon that might have produced the characteristic. In fact, everybody knows what the characteristic is. Out of fear of being held accountable, they refrain from publicly speaking or arguing about it. Indeed, they even deliberately wipe away every trace of it. But it is not only in the corners of the president's eyes. It is also in other parts of his fat, restless body. Even in his dreams. It engenders in everybody who perceives it a tenseness that gradually infects them with the characteristic. They are gradually possessed by it. It is nothing other than brutality.

THE PROFESSOR has been driven mad by the study of butterflies. He is initially committed to the institution, only to be discharged two years later because it has been concluded that his madness is not dangerous to the world. He had the peculiar habit of dancing about the park with a butterfly net, which is a highly amusing sight, for the professor is quite diminutive in stature. He takes hardly any meals, and at his request his room is furnished with a large, black chalkboard on which he writes the word JOY. After he has written the word JOY on the board, he invariably rings for the institution's janitor, who is obliged to erase the word with a large sponge. Each time he receives for his pains a coin from the professor, such that by now he has accumulated a whole bag of these coins. When the professor, to his great sadness, is obliged to leave the institution, he asks for the word JOY to be left on the board. He says he will order the janitor to erase it at a point in time that is still very distant. The staff of the institution are actually quite inconsolable when the professor is picked up and brought to his sister's country estate. He can of course move about quite freely there, but he still lives entirely in his recollection of his residence at the institution. He has long since forgotten everything from before then. Here at the estate, in the summertime, he wears white and cream-coloured clothing. The peasants make fun of him when they see him walking up and down the hill, swinging his butterfly net. But from a certain day onwards he refuses to leave the house except at night, a refusal that his sister and the family doctor, who are dedicating their entire existence to him, have no desire to humour. But he manages to get his way. He says that he wants to catch the lights, every light, for there is nothing more precious than light. That he wants to gather the lights, keep them in a safe place and publish a book about them. So he walks about undisturbed throughout the night every night and catches the lights. One night, he ends up on the train tracks. He holds his butterfly net up to the swiftly enlarging twin lights of the express train. Just before they reach him, he catches them with a swift movement of his tiny clenched hands.

THE BUILDING PAINTER has climbed up a scaffold and realizes that he is some forty or fifty metres above the surface of the earth. He leans against a plank. As he stirs the paint in his bucket with a long strip of pinewood, he looks down at the people who are crowding the street. He tries to pick out some acquaintances of his and even manages to do so, but he has no intention of shouting down at them, for they would then look up at him and find him ridiculous. A ridiculous individual in a dirty yellow uniform and with a hat made out of newspaper on his head! The painter forgets his task and gazes directly down at the black dots. He realizes that he doesn't know anybody who would ever find himself in such a ridiculous situation. If he were fourteen or fifteen years old, sure! But at the age of thirty-two! Throughout this meditation, he is stirring the paint in his bucket. The other painters are much too busy to notice anything about their colleague. A ridiculous individual with a hat made out of newspaper on his head! A ridiculous individual! An appallingly ridiculous individual! Now he feels as though he is rushing and plunging into this meditation, deep into it and down to the bottom of it, in a matter of seconds, and cries of alarm are heard, and when the young man bursts apart on the ground, the people rush away from him centrifugally. They see the overturned bucket fall on him, and the painter is immediately covered in spilled yellow exterior paint. Now the passers-by raise their heads. But of course the painter is no longer up above.

THE MONEY POSTMAN* flees with his full leather satchel across the border. He swims across the river and saves himself from drowning by climbing onto a stump of a bough protruding from the undergrowth. He removes his shoes and roams through the woods barefoot. The farther away from his village he gets, the gloomier the landscape becomes. Eventually, he is at the mercy of the darkness. He is obliged to crawl across long expanses of mossy ground and skins his knees. By his reckoning, the sun must have long since risen. But the darkness remains statically in place. Even the cries he emits while sitting on a fallen tree trunk receive no echo. Then he suddenly realizes: *I'm not allowed to scream*! He sees a light, the outline of a farmhouse. He approaches it, dragging the satchel along behind him. He snaps the satchel open and shut and trudges forward once again. He thinks: *I'm not allowed to go in there*! Hunger begins its work, making him feverish and eventually throwing him into a ditch. Before impact he wakes up and realizes that the whole thing was only a dream of which nothing remains but his feverish body. He gets up and goes out. He takes a walk and doesn't go back to bed till four in the morning. But the next day he resigns from his position as money postman and has himself transferred. He tells his wife that he would rather live in town, around lots of people, that the darkness wouldn't be as dark there.

---

* In German-speaking countries, *Geldbriefträger*—through the end of the twentieth century, a postman entrusted exclusively with delivering money in various forms, chiefly postal money orders. [Trans.]

THE PLATELAYER, who for seventeen years has been doing his job to the satisfaction of his supervisors and with his savings has built himself a small house beneath the railway embankment, discovers on his way home through the goods yard an open refrigerator car in which some slaughtered pigs are hanging. As there is no sign of any of the Customs officers who are otherwise always standing around the cars, and as his curiosity is now piqued, he climbs into the car to learn how cold it is in there through his own skin. He sits down on the plank that spans the floor and falls asleep. Because the man is sitting in a corner that cannot be seen by the Customs officers, he is not discovered by them, and they seal up the door after they have carried out their inspection and before the platelayer has climbed out. Four days later, at the train's destination, the platelayer is found dead in the midst of the pig carcasses and sitting on the plank. At first the people who find him believe that he froze to death, but then they discover that the man, who has nothing on his person but his work uniform and whom they consequently cannot identify, can hardly have frozen to death, as the car's refrigerating mechanism has broken down and closer scrutiny reveals that the pork is spoiled and inedible. The men who transport the deceased to the loading dock for temporary storage conjecture that in his terror at the thought of never getting out of the car and of inevitably freezing to death, he had a stroke.

THE INNKEEPER, along with his wife and his two sisters, is in the vestibule of his inn and busily stuffing blood-sausage filling into a long pig intestine and hanging the resulting string of blood sausages up to dry. Thanks to the inclusion of barley meal in the filling, he has managed to tie off more than his permitted number of blood sausages, but nobody finds out about this. After the work is over and the last traces of the butchery, which has lasted all day, have been washed away, he sends the others off to bed. As he is taking in some fresh air in the front doorway and thinking out his plan, his strategy, for dinner at this Sunday's after-church party, which he is going to host on the front lawn of his inn, he is approached by a drunkard who informs him of his intention to kill himself. He is going to hang himself from the nearest tree, he says. The innkeeper laughs at this, shuts the front door and retires for the night. Next morning, as he is dragging two of the wooden sides of the shooting gallery onto the lawn, he discovers the drunkard from the previous evening on one of his apple trees. He did in fact hang himself. But since the after-church party must take place there on Sunday, the innkeeper does not run to the local constable to tell him about the incident; rather, he cuts the corpse from the tree and lets it fall onto the grass. He harnesses a horse and carries the corpse to the hay trailer. With swiftly attained decisiveness, he drives the corpse into the woods a half an hour from his house. He fastens an iron wheel to the dead body and drops it into a pond just beyond the woods. This having been done, the after-church party can take place without disruption. Between the shooting gallery and the free food, the people have a good time. Nobody learns anything conclusive from the neighbouring parish about the drunkard, who is indeed the object of a multi-day search but is also forgotten soon afterwards.

A MACHINE that is like a guillotine is slicing off large pieces of a slowly advancing mass of rubber and letting them fall onto a conveyor belt which is advancing one level below and at which are seated female workers who have to inspect the sliced-off pieces and eventually pack them up in large cardboard boxes. The machine has been in operation for only nine weeks, and the day on which it was delivered to the management of the factory will never be forgotten by anyone who was present at that ceremony. It had been brought to the factory in a train car specially constructed for it, and the day's official speaker emphatically asserted that this machine represented one of the greatest technological achievements of all time. Its arrival at the factory was greeted by a brass band, and the workers and the engineers welcomed it with doffed hats. Its installation took a fortnight, and its owners were able to assure themselves of its efficiency and reliability. It simply has to be lubricated regularly, and naturally, every fortnight, with special oils. The lubrication requires one of the female workers to climb a steel spiral staircase and slowly release the oil through a valve. This worker is thoroughly briefed down to the smallest detail of the operation. In spite of this, the girl loses her footing in such an unfortunate way as to end up decapitated. Her head tumbles down onto the conveyor belt like the pieces of rubber. The female workers who are sitting at the conveyor belt are so horrified that not one of them can cry out. They deal with the girl's head in the usual way they deal with the pieces of rubber. The woman at the end of the line picks up the head and packs it up in a box.

THE YOUNG MAN is trying to prove to an old man that he, *the young man*, is alone. He tells him that he came to the city to get to know people but has so far not succeeded in getting to know them or even in making even a single human acquaintance. That he has tried to win people's trust by various means. But that he has repelled them. To be sure, he says, they have let him say his piece and even listened to him, but they haven't wanted to *understand* him. He says that he has brought them presents, because with presents it is possible to elicit people's friendship and devotion. But that they have rejected the presents and shown him the door. He says that for days on end he has been pondering why they have not wanted to have anything to do with him. But that he has not managed to figure this out. He says that he has even *metamorphosed* himself to win people over; that he has been one individual after another and played these roles convincingly, but that even by this means he has not won over a single human being. He speaks so vehemently to the old man, who is sitting beside the front door of his house, that he suddenly feels embarrassed. He takes a step back and notices that nothing is going on inside the old man. Inside the old man there is nothing perceptible to him. Now the young man runs to his room and tucks himself into bed.

THE STAR PUPIL, whose life is more methodical than the life of grownups, dreams that he cannot solve a mathematical problem and that the problem remains unsolved when the teacher orders the pupils to turn in their assignments. The teacher takes the star pupil to task during class and threatens to inform his parents of the incident. His schoolmates are brimming over with *schadenfreude* and push the star pupil, who is a physical weakling, into a canal that he manages to get out of only with the utmost effort. The next day, he does not dare to enter the school and remains standing at its front gate for ten minutes after the start of class. He turns around and plays truant. He runs around in a park and there is discovered by the school's janitor, who reports the incident to the administration. Now the star pupil awakens from his dream. He rushes sweating and half-naked into his parents' bedroom. But no matter how searchingly and inventively they question him, he does not tell them what his dream was about. Time and again he refuses to talk about it.

BEINGS OF SUPERIOR STRENGTH order him to read a fairly lengthy paragraph in a book, a paragraph that he cannot understand because he has not worked out what the paragraph says. And even though they keep telling him that the content of the paragraph is simple and that accordingly he must understand it, he has no idea where to begin with the argument propounded in it. Consequently, they send him to another room, where he has to answer various questions, which he finds easy to do, for the questions are phrased like questions he could have posed to the questioners himself. Eventually, however, the most important question comes, and even though he makes a great effort to answer it, he finds it impossible to do so. The beings of superior strength let him have the interval between the eleventh and the thirteenth hour; then they resolve to declare the question unanswered. They send him to another floor for a solution to his problem. They mentioned to him a door number for which he now searches. He searches for hours on end, and when he collapses from sheer fatigue, he starts searching again because he has no option but to search for the door number. Eventually, he faints. He comes to, continues his search for the door number. By now he is on the thirty-fourth floor, and he has still not found the door number. The corridors are long. At an indeterminable point, they peter out in darkness. So it takes him days to reach the sixty-ninth floor. But even on the seventieth floor and on the seventy-fifth, he does not find the door number, although the higher he climbs, the likelihood of his finding the door number is constantly increasing. Any door may turn out to supply the sought-after number. He casts off his clothes to move forward more swiftly. He works out a feasible method of taking in two or even three door numbers at a glance. A fantasy that he is constantly dosing himself with narcotics gives him undreamt-of energy between the ninety-ninth and one-hundred-and-tenth floors. On the one-hundred-and-fifteenth floor, he collapses. But a voice that passes itself off as that of a human being tells him that there are only four more floors in this building. And so he struggles to his feet and covers the remaining distance. By the time he has reached the last door number, he is convinced that the number that the beings of superior strength mentioned to him does not even exist. In reality, he has forgotten it. Out of fear that the beings of superior strength will think he is crazy, he remains on the top floor and hides behind a dustbin. He is discovered there only months later.

THE GOVERNMENT CLERK is referring to a male voice that he heard on the approach to the bridge when he was about to go home. This voice, he says, urged him to perform the act known as a crime. 'This voice was so insistent that I was at its mercy. But perhaps you do not know, gentlemen, what it is like to be under the control of such a voice. These voices catch one completely unawares.' He describes his route home in all its particulars. Yes, he says to himself, I must tell them about this and also about that, and I mustn't forget the smallest detail. One sees in his face the enormous strain that his effort to remember everything is causing him. People like him, members of the lower civil service, appear in court every day, and it is the very precision of their testimony that bores their listeners. The clerk says that he never wanted his life in the first place, 'but in the end, once one has taken on and taken up something, one can't just turn around and destroy it, simply demolish it.' As a child, he was always at a disadvantage. Naturally, he tried through exceptional attentiveness to win the friendship of his teachers, but over time these efforts turned out to be pointless. He ended up in a governmental office and grew old. He got married because his co-workers of the same age and classification as him had got married, and he lost his wife thanks to the inattentiveness of a motorist. He describes how he tried to snatch the briefcase from the elderly man. 'I believe,' he says, 'that when the actual moment came for me to take the briefcase and run away, I no longer wanted to do it at all. I never wanted to do it. Never,' he said. 'But the man refused to be convinced of this. He shouted. He did nothing but shout. And even though I could have run away, I stayed put. Isn't that sufficient proof of my innocence? It was as if I had suddenly become a part of this man. I told the man why I wasn't about to run away, but he wouldn't listen. Your Honours, what I am saying is true. It is all true! And even if it could be a lie, it is true. Moreover, gentlemen,' he says, 'I happen by nature to be a good man, perhaps less a good man than an irreproachable one. Please bear that in mind.' The court has no sympathy for him and even less for a male voice that it believes the accused has made up. The court sentences him to twenty years in prison. To the maximum term, for the crime in question was obviously a robbery.

THE CHIMNEY-SWEEP, who has been living in the village for forty years—but who throughout this period has remained an outsider whom none of the farmers, nor even a single one of the other villagers, takes seriously, because he has not managed to acquire even the tiniest parcel of officially registered land—is on his way home from a tavern at which a drinking spree has taken place. He is so drunk that he has lost his way and is walking in a direction diametrically opposite to that of his dwelling. At the site of the milk table on which in the early morning the farmers set the milk cans for the dairy van, he slips out of his coat and casts it off. A couple of paces farther on, he makes a discovery that stops him in his tracks. In the middle of the road, he discovers a man who is undoubtedly dead. The chimney-sweep does not notice this and bends over him. He addresses him as though the dead man, a farmer who has had a stroke on his way home, is his best friend, and he kisses the dead man and says that he is glad to have found him, that he is no longer afraid, for until then he was afraid. 'Nobody wants me,' he says. He adds that the man lying on the ground is well disposed towards him. That nobody else is. Actually, the chimney-sweep knows the dead man. He says his name. He reels around him a couple of times; then he pulls him so far along the edge of the road that the dead man rolls into the brook. He is now completely wrapped in snow. He will lie down next to him, he says, and sleep with him. He does just that. He lies down next to him and presses his warm body against the already frozen-stiff other one. He falls asleep immediately.

THE DROVER on his way to T. imagines that he is in a position to buy up all the cattle in the province. He suddenly pictures the other drovers driving cattle from every corner of the province and himself sitting and buying at its centre. He is sitting on a three-legged stool. Eventually, the cattle owners even come to sell him their livestock in person. They no longer treat him like a completely ordinary drover, as they always have done until now: they even invite him to their elegant houses. He has rented a large pen in which he can house the cattle. He has also hired farmhands who have to feed the cattle, to milk the cows. Finally, nobody brings him any cattle any longer, because he is now in possession of every single head of cattle in the province. There is not a single head of cattle in a single barn, everybody says. This proves that he is the richest person in the province. Suddenly, the densely packed cattle grow restless, and they recognize the drover as the being responsible for the terrible situation in which they find themselves. Soon the farmhands with the feed are no longer able to force their way into the pent-up herd, which is unmistakably huge, and the cattle get hungry and revolt and band together. At the moment at which the bloated bellies of two of his cows are crushing to a pulp the already insensible drover, he again sees before him the town of T., which he must drive into, and to the rump of the cow or bull in front of him, which is plodding along the torrid country highway towards the town, he delivers a thump that causes the animal to emit a pain-deadening noise.

THE TOBACCONIST is gazing out of her kiosk on the square, which is sited between the canal and the cemetery wall, and in which twice a day large crowds of workers in grey overalls band together and wait for buses. It is six o'clock in the evening, and utterly void of people though the square is right now, it will be chock-full of them and suffocatingly grey in six or seven minutes. The flood of workers will pour out and inundate the square. The shop will jut out of the grey mass like an island. The younger workers will be the first ones, the old ones the last. In the course of thirteen years the view through her tiny shop window has not changed. She takes a packet of tobacco down from the shelf and shoves it under the counter. Then she digs her round, bloated face into the pits of her elbows and looks over at the tall tree that juts up into the sky, but she cannot see that it does. Her round breasts are held back by the fabric of her blouse; one gets the feeling that they are bound to ooze out at any moment. In this soundless attitude, the tobacconist awaits the arrival of her lover. Like all the others, he is employed at the factory. He is about twenty years older, even fatter, even more bloated. At the sight of this image, which she beholds steaming in the square as if enveloped in fog, she is seized by a fit of nausea. For a while she contemplates everything even more intensively without stirring. But then, suddenly, in violation of the rules, she lowers the roller blind, pulls the cash drawer out of the register, circumspectly places it in her shopping bag and leaves the kiosk. She flies across the bridge and from there runs through the alleyways. The foul stench of the workers, which is now streaming from every opening behind her, makes her gag on the nausea in her throat.

THE HEADMASTER summons the teacher into his presence and accuses him of having sexually abused one of his pupils. The headmaster says that he does not know what he should say but that the teacher's transfer to another village is absolutely necessary. But, the headmaster adds, he will probably even have to give up his career as a teacher. In any case, says the headmaster, he must make a report to the district superintendent of schools and the whole affair will have much grimmer repercussions even than those just disclosed. The teacher makes no attempt whatsoever to explain himself; he merely asserts that he has not abused the pupil, that the very idea of committing an act such as the one described by the headmaster (for the headmaster has been unable to refrain from describing it in detail) never would have crossed his mind. But no matter how firmly the teacher denies the accusation, it is no use. The headmaster says he is suspended from service effective immediately and dismisses him without offering him his hand as he has always done till today. Because the teacher is conscious of no guilt, he thinks that in time his innocence will come to light and that he will quite simply treat his suspension as a leave of absence. That the rumour will never even spread beyond the school. But he is mistaken. The rumour spreads like wildfire, and even the town's newspaper reports on it. The paper maintains that a man like the teacher ought to be put behind bars. That no punishment could be too severe for him. That young people, and above all children, must be protected from him by hook or by crook. Because the teacher has recently married, the affair is doubly unpleasant for him. His wife does not believe him and leaves him when she hears of the accusation. Only a few days after his suspension, the teacher receives a subpoena from the district court. Nobody knows what he is up to in the days preceding the hearing; in any case, he no longer shows his face in public. By then nobody is any longer unfamiliar with his story. His landlady insists on his moving out and gives him back the cheque with which he has paid his rent in advance. A day before the hearing, his body is found in a river that is on the verge of flooding, seventeen kilometres from the town where he lived. It turns out that he most certainly did not commit suicide but instead had the misfortune of falling into the river and drowning. Now the pupil comes forward and says that the whole story is a lie, that he made it up to get even with the young teacher.

THE DICTATOR has selected a shoe shiner from a pool of over a hundred applicants. He entrusts him with no other duty than shining his shoes. This suits the simple man from the countryside to the ground, and he swiftly puts on weight, and over the years he and his superior—and he is subordinate to no one but the dictator—gradually become virtual spitting images of each other. Perhaps this is partly owing to the fact that the shoe shiner eats the same food as the dictator. Soon he has acquired the same fat nose, and once he has lost his hair, the same bald pate. A pair of thick lips appear, and when he grins he displays his teeth. Everybody, even the cabinet ministers and the dictator's most intimate confidants, is afraid of the shoe shiner. In the evening, he crosses his booted legs and plays a musical instrument. He writes long letters to his family who spread his fame throughout the countryside. 'When you're the dictator's shoe shiner,' they say, 'you're closer to the dictator than anybody else.' The shoe shiner is quite literally closer to the dictator than anybody else, for he always has to sit just outside his bedroom and even to sleep there. He is not allowed to leave his post under any circumstances. One night, though, when he feels strong enough, he enters the room without warning, wakes the dictator up, and striking him down with his fist, renders him stone dead in bed. The shoe shiner quickly takes off his clothes, slips them onto the dead dictator and dons the dictator's uniform. While standing in front of the dictator's mirror, he notices that he really does look like the dictator. Without a moment's hesitation, he runs out of the room and cries out that his shoe shiner has suddenly attacked him. That in self-defence he has struck him down and killed him. That the shoe shiner should be taken away and his survivors notified.

THE MANOR HOUSE is the setting of an important christening ceremony that may safely be described as a celebration. The landed gentry, timber merchants and common people from all over the province gather there. Even fireworks explode over the woods, immersing the landscape in a harmless thunderstorm-like atmosphere for several minutes. Flashes of lightning shred the contours of the forest. Enormous quantities of champagne and wine, brandy and French cognac, were already being transported to the spot shortly after midday. A chef who is herself a baroness has designed and cooked a dinner appropriate to the hot weather and sliced up a mountain of white bread. A brass band has set up in the park that stretches from the stately residence down to the riverbank. If they are indeed the same ensemble whom one invariably encounters on such occasions, the spectacle they are capable of producing would be bound to delight any onlooker who should happen to behold it from a bird's-eye view. The celebration, which began at seven o'clock in the evening, and to which a magician and a poet have contributed their distinctive shares, culminates at eleven-thirty with the appearance of the young mother, who has spent the entire day next door at the steward's estate with her husband. The christening, which as it is winding down is still being described as the most successful in the entire province, ends at four in the morning. At this moment, in the small room in front of the acorn tree, the young mother notices that her newborn son is lying asphyxiated under a heavy damask blanket. The infant's nurse is to blame.

THE SACRISTAN standing before the altar keeps catching sight of himself in the choir stalls. Each time he lights the candles, his own gaunt figure is sandwiched between the pillars. He runs towards it. By the time has reached it, the image has vanished. After Mass, it is the same. The people are gone, he extinguishes the candles and he sees himself walking over the tops of the rows of pews. This figure, this figure of himself, makes him so anxious that he falls down weeping at the foot of the altar. But he never talks about his experience. Not even to his wife, who has been bedridden for years, does he so much as drop a hint about it. And yet he cannot completely conceal it. Everybody notices that something has changed. They can see that he is getting even thinner, and while playing cards he makes mistakes that nobody makes. In the afternoons, he locks himself away and pores over the old newspapers that the resident priest leaves for him in the vestibule from time to time. His wife encounters him only at mealtimes, but she is like all wives; she does not draw his attention to his affliction; although she does not know what it is, she tries to avoid reminding him of it. On Easter Sunday he suddenly receives a blow on the head from this figure, which he ever more clearly recognizes as himself, and tumbles to the floor. Before even the first members of the congregation arrive, he manages to stand up. On the crown of his head is a warm bloodstain. He is obliged to bandage his head. The priest asks him what happened to him, and he replies: 'I fell down.' He slipped, he says. A few days after Easter, some members of the congregation find him dead with his head split open. To this day nobody knows who killed him, for nobody harbours so much as the faintest suspicion of anybody else or of himself.

THE STEWARDESS OF THE LADY OF A MANOR is accused by her of having stolen at least forty eggs. She denies this and says that she has stolen not a single egg. That she had 'no need whatsoever to steal even one egg'. That she buys her eggs in town. She wonders, she says, how the lady ever could have alighted on the idea of suspecting her, accusing her, in such a base and shabby manner. She says that she has worked for her for twenty years and has 'always had to work very hard.' That in all these twenty years this has never happened. And that now she, her mistress, suddenly suspects her of having stolen eggs. At night, the stewardess gets even with the lady by decapitating all the flowers in the garden of the manor.

A HANDFUL OF PEOPLE are obliged to dig a grave, and their digging is supervised by two soldiers with one machine gun between them. The supervised are members of a family with a famous name, a name that means nothing to the two uniformed men who are following all their movements with unremitting attention. It is four in the morning and cold. The woods cast a large arm-shaped shadow across the grave which is swiftly getting bigger, because both the soldiers are impatient. The entire scene unfolds in silence. Only the shovels and the clods of earth that keep rolling off the mound beside the grave are audible. When the grave is big enough, the people who have dug it are obliged to station themselves at its edge with their backs to the woods. They are shot dead by the machine gun and successively fall face-first into the grave. Shortly afterwards, an officer appears with a group of six soldiers. Now the two men who shot the civilians into the grave are compelled to station themselves at the edge of the grave like their victims and are struck down. Shortly afterwards the sun rises, the slain are covered in shovelfuls of earth and the setting is completely bereft of all human presence.

THE CUSTOMS COLLECTOR is made fun of by the children of the town on account of his diminutive stature. The children shout terms of abuse at him; while crouching up in the trees, they pelt him so hard with chestnuts that he often writhes in pain on his cot. He is affable. If he had longer legs and a bigger torso, he would be popular with everybody. For all that, he has been keeping more and more to himself and spending his free time not in town but either with comrades or alone in the garden of the Customs house. At a certain point in time, he began hatching some unusual idea and keeping it a secret, for as he tells himself, one ought to keep one's most brilliant flashes of insight to oneself. Overnight he procured himself an army—not an army compelled to serve him but an enemy army. It is composed of the trees that line the avenue leading to the custom-booth on the bridge, of the *willow column*, of the *fern formation*, of the *snake-plant unit*. It is not easy for him to expose himself unobtrusively to such a mighty enemy host each day. But it is precisely this strategy, which costs him the better part of his energy, that he requires; no other will do. He talks about it in his dreams, but the other Customs collectors have no idea what he is talking about. They notice that he needs them less than he used to. He has completely given up visiting the town. He is now only ever seen in the avenue, amid the willows, amid the ferns, amid the snake plants. In their midst, he comports himself like Alexander, like Napoleon. In the evening, he eats a great deal and gets fat. One day, the Customs collector becomes so excited he loses control, and he raises his revolver and wildly shoots down one tree on the avenue after another until he runs out of bullets. As all this has taken place in full view of the other Customs collectors, they take the weapon away from him and lock him in the cell in the Customs house. Late that night, he is hauled off by two men in military overcoats.

THE SURVIVOR NOTES: towards the end of the war, both of the city's hills have tunnels drilled into them, tunnels into which the people stream because they are threatened with annihilation. Only because they go into the tunnels do they get through the war alive. At first, they do not venture into the light of day. Only hesitantly do they let those whom they regard as weak and worthless step outside the gates; eventually, they also let the children out, and in the afternoon they all silently leave the tunnels in which many of them have asphyxiated because they had too little oxygen. They voluntarily haul out the dead and unceremoniously bury them just outside the exits. But now that the war is over, something happens that nobody can comprehend: by sheer force of habit, instead of filling in the tunnels, they enter them. They do this every day at the same hour. As long as they live, they will keep going into the tunnels.

A CLOUDBURST* sets in motion colossal masses of stone and buries a three hundred-metre stretch of the railway line that runs along the riverbed and through the cutting in the mountain rock. Eventually, thousands of logs completely block the opening of the valley, and the water from the river spreads over the entire valley and floods the line-keeper's lodge in which the line-keeper and his wife are fast asleep. The flood sweeps away the building and submerges it in the river, such that even after the water level has returned to normal, it cannot be found. The catastrophe has not left a single trace of the line-keeper's lodge or its inhabitants. Within a few hours of the terrible disaster, hundreds of workers have begun the clean-up operation. At night, they work with the aid of floodlights. The entire province takes part in this project. Because the line is one of the most important transportation routes in the country, special troops from the capital have been drafted for the project. Suddenly the peaceful valley formerly

---

* This story and the following one (A STRANGER) originally formed part of *Ereignisse*, and in 1959 were published in the magazine *Wort in der Zeit* alongside early versions of four other stories (A PLATELAYER, THE MANOR HOUSE, THE HEADMASTER and AN ACTOR) from the collection, but were ultimately excluded from the published volume. [Trans. after Bernhard's editors]

populated solely by mountain farmers and small-time craftsmen is overrun by rubber-raincoat-enveloped men compressed by large, flat steel helmets. But after a mere seven weeks instead of the scheduled thirteen, train service is restored to the line. This is the occasion of a large if peculiar festival attended by several cabinet ministers. Beside the monument to the workers who gave their lives during the difficult original construction project, a second smaller monument to the unfortunate and never-discovered line-keeping couple is erected. In fact, this entire story is a dream from which the dreamer is awoken by the shutting of his bedroom door. As he is passing by the line-keeper's lodge in the morning, he remembers his dream, and although he sees the line-keeper just as he is lowering the crossing barrier, he knows full well that it is a dead man who will be raising the barrier again a couple of minutes later.

A STRANGER has himself announced as a refugee at an estate one evening. The estate is the one in which the prince spends several weeks each summer with his family and from which he exerts a considerable influence on the politics of the national government, to which he belongs and is obligated as a member of its parliament. The stranger is invited to a conference with the prince, which causes quite a stir in the house. The prince appears and asks the stranger to be seated. He has him tell him about his escape and about the conditions that prevail in his country overrun by invaders. He listens attentively and paces nervously up and down the room while outside a storm rages violently but to no possible detrimental effect on this magnificent abode, for it has metre-thick walls and was designed with great skill by its architect. The prince asks a few questions, which the stranger answers. He wins the trust of the prince, who offers him a position on his estate, a position commensurate with his rank, of which the stranger has spoken. He becomes the steward of the estate, which is possible only because the former steward was unmasked as a traitor and put to death. After a half-hour conference with the stranger, the prince leaves the room. An hour later, they are dining in the large drawing room with the princess and a visiting foreigner, for today is a holiday about which the stranger knows nothing, and nobody even tells him what event is being commemorated by it. During the meal, the stranger commits a blunder. This blunder, a slight peculiarity in the way he eats his food, betrays him. Even before the next day dawns he is shot to death by the prince's bodyguards and unceremoniously buried in a plot of land near the border.

A Springtime

How everything withdraws from one, how anguish becomes anguish anew, how darkness becomes lethal anew, how fortifications like human beings fall to pieces, how you are gazing into your toothless age, is being pointed up by this springtime; you can get up whenever you choose, you can go wherever you choose, but this springtime with its cataclysmic storms is wiping you away, shovelling you over to the side of the road . . . hissing you into the remotest corner, from one periphery into the next, from the philosophical periphery into the cringing, canine periphery, from the cringing, canine periphery into the laughable, pitiful periphery . . . once again all the lodgers in all the flophouses are giving themselves the lie; they are drawing together their curtains, their qualms ridden with queasiness . . . from the melancholy of the warmed-over sexes the almighty sex crime of death is once again emerging; once again, terrified into million-fold astonishment, they are vomiting at the sight of the begrimed, snow-forsaken

---

Originally published in 1963 as 'Ein Frühling' in the trade anthology *Spektrum des Geistes 1964. Literaturkalendar* to introduce readers to Bernhard in connection with the publication of his first novel, *Frost*. [Trans. after Bernhard's editors]

corpse . . . entire regions are suddenly displaying their ulcers, overflowing river courses are heralding the end of the close season, files are being leafed through again, everybody is being harangued, condemned, by the presiding judges; weariness is being decapitated; everywhere once again there is this stupid procreative confidentiality in the upper and the lower echelons; the world is once again standing united in this boundless villainous exhibitionism on behalf of its principles . . . In the torrent of theories you behold how the orders are subordinating themselves, how the detritus of the years is bedimming your eyesight, how ideas are being torn to pieces, how words are crumbling to pieces. Here in the great cemeteries of all the blocks of all the streets you are studying the great book reviews of heaven, in every figure of speech you uncover a legion of felonies, a legion of habitual felonies . . . in these colossal waiting rooms a single word, a mere fit of a thought, the mere attempt to escape for even a moment, suffices to ruin whoever is sitting in them . . . everyone and everything have been exhausted by this judgement, have fled in countless numbers down into the base swamplands of vulgar bellyaching, into the nagging uncertainty of dreams . . . You are ridiculed by the unintelligibility of intelligence, by the dictatorship of the creative debaser . . . you leaf through their meaningless books, you are no longer investigating anything . . . you no longer make yourself intelligible; you never place any trust in them and in their incurable decline, in their socially toxic intellectual leprosy . . . Alone in the homelessness of your thoughts you no longer consist of anything but hunger and thirst amid the eternal unintelligibility of the stars

. . . in this springtime everything and all things are once again at their end; like tomorrow and the day after tomorrow, they are founded on misunderstandings, on a million sterile constellations, on the frugality of nature, which is a mighty stoppage of unrest, a colossal silencing, a silencing of the composition of the air and of the sturdiness and ruthlessness of metals against all memories . . . this springtime, in which nature is *daring* to reinvent human existence, is a universally lethal deafening odour of the millennia.

(*from the author's first notebook*)

A Witness' Testimony

I moved from a First Class compartment to a Second Class compartment and then back to a First Class compartment; like my father, I was constantly changing places; I was fretful; I am ill, I was trying to find an entirely ordinary peaceful place so that I could jot down my notes, those remarks that I told you about earlier, those brief snatches of reminiscence; soon it will be winter; then it will no longer be possible for me to jot down these notes; the arduousness of my work as a clinician will make it impossible for me to write down even a single sentence, and so I sought out an auspicious place; for my purposes I need a place that I can obscure, obnubilate, as I see fit . . . but people have an aversion to darkness; for some inexplicable reason, they dread darkness; even quite seasoned travellers dread it . . . all the while I was busy studying the most dissimilar characters, the individualistic types and the mass types; I fairly felt duty-bound to construct them, to reconstruct them day after day for my purposes; I step into

---

Originally published in the October 1963 issue of *Das Inselschiff*, a promotional periodical issued by Insel, the publishers of *Frost*. [Trans. after Bernhard's editors]

human beings, into their secret, inconspicuous processes of decomposition; as one steps into cities, I step into human beings; I harbour no dread of this humiliating act; a colossal misconception of all sciences enables me to step into human beings . . . until I suddenly stand aghast in the midst of the fantastic geometry of disagreements, of the queasiness of two millennia, where concepts stand on their heads like nightmares, until finally, all at once, triumphing over each and every acrobatic feint, I descry in my ruined brain the untruthfulness of my own truth . . . all of this is of course very perplexing, but you have of course ordered me to describe my encounter with the murderer, that encounter that I shall never forget; I never forget any encounter, not even the most insignificant one; that is indeed the most terrifying aspect of my disposition, the lethal element of my nature; that is indeed the colossally monstrous facet of my essence! I suppose I am a person possessed of a refined version of all instinctual capabilities, a person removed from pure scientific observation, a person given to exercising great liberty, the utmost degree of liberty, the most profound, the most radical liberty imaginable, a person who time and again, day after day, is striding deep into the accursed physicality of thoughts, into the gargantuan amorphousness of emotions . . . at bottom, my calculations are singularly situated within the ambit of both opinions and laws . . . wherever I go, I think only of the immense quantity of academies, convocations, associations, of those enormous heaps of perfidious lineage with their noisome applause; the truth is that *I*, in the light of the world as such, am founded on a misconception, on the greatest of all the misconceptions with which I have personally become acquainted, of all the misconceptions I have personally if inadvertently generated in the course of time, I suppose I can say that my glory is that nothing is . . . because everything is founded on a misconception, a misconception contained in the history compiled from millions of seemingly—mind you, *seemingly*—crazed brains; for years, I have been working on an *essay about misconceptions*, about the general misconceptions of our age, about the misconceptions of all ages, of all of history, of all events, of all thoughts, of all phenomena, of the uphill and downhill development of the world; the world is a world that is constantly involved in the untruth of evanescent lethal procedures . . . one afternoon, at the age of thirty, in my uncle's house at the timberline of the Limestone Alps, I suddenly began to study the sufferings of my generation, to try to exhaust these sufferings and explain them to myself by looking at the graves, at the graves of the war and at the graves of the air, at the graves of millions of thoughts; I managed to pursue this flash of inspiration in unlimited security, and it preoccupied me for an entire decade, but the deeper I penetrated into this thought, I always remained merely in touch with it, merely in touch with this thought, with this world, with this air, with this generation . . . I was just writing something about the general human condition, about the imperfection of everything divine, when I was obliged to leave the compartment; a gentleman and a lady—presumably they were travelling a much longer distance than me—chased me out; I now precisely recall a cursory inspection of their suitcases, of their clothing; the gentleman uttered a succession of sonorous sentences amounting to an admittedly clear but completely political stream of nonsense, the lady spoke incessantly of a rampaging shark offshore . . . with the utmost intensity I studied the gentleman's footwear, the lady's jewellery; noisily, an insignificant child of his social class, he slept; the lady occasionally asked, 'Where are we?,' expressing the unreliability of woman, of her sex, a truly disconnected object of desire; in the corridor I went on to think: people don't belong together, they belong only apart, just as everything belongs only apart; nature, that wedge between the sexes . . . the smell of people, of railway people, of travelling people . . . I am constantly colliding with a person; it is of course precisely what one dreads most that happens to one, precisely this appalling ugliness, this egregious treachery . . . I had an altercation with the waiter; he had begrimed my trousers, suddenly begrimed them; instead of begging my pardon, he assailed me with terms of abuse; people hurl their terms of abuse in my face; in fine and in short, I went into the dining car; I took a seat as far away as possible from the kitchen, at a window . . . that wasteland of a landscape, those monotonous colours, those ridiculous experiments of mindless economization . . . I no longer remember what I ordered; butter, bread, water; at bottom, I preoccupied myself with the *problem of urgency*, with the *causes of existence*, I tried to work out how numerous the individual is in reality, outside of every truth; an attempt that was bound to miscarry, as all attempts are bound to miscarry; one problem pulls the next one up out of the water and throws it back in; all problems are incessantly undergoing death by drowning, death by asphyxiation . . . I aimed at a million targets simultaneously . . . suddenly I was startled by an incivility; I stood up and paid my bill and walked through the car and looked for my compartment; I senselessly went in the wrong direction, I was heading, while thinking those thoughts, towards the end of the train, not towards the engine . . . the lady kept spitefully opening the window, even though I kept shutting it . . . the man, the gentleman, also a symbol of solitude, said: 'The power struggles!' . . . you may picture to yourself a middling civil servant who travels to the opening of every session of Parliament, an absolutely revolting, ridiculous, emphatically pitiful apparition; I saw a rather large number of cows standing in the rain, one of those particulars that inspire sudden, brief bursts of confidence; all of a sudden I saw the countryside; after the appalling wasteland with its ordered organization I saw variety, disorganization, all of it seemingly mere semblance; waterfalls and gorges, the evening; you know what that means: I suddenly saw the evening . . . all those people exuded a pitiful solitariness, a mendacious, putrid parochialism; through a forest of malodorous clothes, of stupid faces, I flogged myself through the cars, through all those ancient, dilapidated railway cars; everywhere I went I encountered the stench of urine, the din of doors that no longer shut properly, of cracked windows; everywhere I encountered discarded scraps of paper, waves of remorseless sweat...it suddenly struck me that this was nothing less than felonious, that the phrase 'ascertainment of truth' was felonious; I experienced an appalling feeling of queasiness on thinking of the phrase 'true sentence', of the word 'elementary' . . . I thought to myself that man is by no means knowingly a construction; that he himself is not; that he is not himself without himself, nor himself with himself and in himself; indeed, that man by no means is and is not nothing; by no means can he be nothing and yet he is not, because it is not true that he was not and cannot be, that he cannot be spontaneously . . . I felt as though I had been delivered up to the ordeal of these researches, to all even merely imaginable books, all imaginable explanations, influences, arithmetics, balancing acts of mathematics . . . perhaps it is true that I walked all the way to the end of the train, that *may* very well be true, but I cannot remember; in one fully occupied compartment I saw a thin, grey, intelligent, moribund face, a face that had long since ceased to engender confidence; such types die off even before they have come to maturity . . . the intellect dislodges them, the intellect perforates them . . . I have become acquainted and lost touch with a succession of such types, lost touch with something of which I know nothing, be it a country, be it a mountain . . . in all these interconnections, the concept of 'creation' avows its own incompetence, everything is going under with concepts and yet, as I know for a fact, consensus persists . . . the young man is astonished at what the old man actuates with the word 'hypothesis' . . . synthesis, parenthesis . . . logic, the sister of the big sister of the laws of gravity, is a phenomenon like truth, like untruth, nothing but disruption . . . old age is always only a witness of quite grand execution ceremonies . . . everything is being executed, all these people are constantly living in the consciousness of being obliged to die away, to vanish; it is also true that once one has attained adulthood everything turns to rot; suddenly people learn to inhale everything in the form of rot, to exhale everything in the form of rot; suddenly the more intelligent among them descry the all-destroying symptom of rot in everyone and everything . . . everyone speaks, talks, moans, wheezes, swears nothing but rot . . . I remember I was already at the station an hour before the departure of the train; after that third sleepless night, I could no longer bear being in my room; I organized my papers; I shipped off my books; I organized, organized and thereby procured myself the greatest disorganization imaginable; I did not eat breakfast; I did not eat anything at lunchtime either; I ran all over town for such a long time, to the government offices, to the houseware stores, across the river and back, into the park and back out of it, into the lower streets, into the upper streets; all of a sudden I no longer knew where I was; this of course is also a consequence of my appalling sleep deprivation; I get every name wrong, get wrong every person, every impression, everything of any importance . . . so then I had finally fled to the train station; at the train station, I thought, I shall manage to calm down . . . but in that silence that prevailed at the train station, in the train cars and on the platforms—not a single arriving train was in sight or earshot, nor a single departing one—I started clinically suffocating; I realized all of a sudden what a terrible mistake it was to believe that repose was what I was looking for; for somebody like me, repose is of course the greatest of tormentors, the most horrible of punishments, the greatest of felonesses . . . how glad I was to hear the first passengers walking through the car, to hear running feet, to hear laughter, to hear weeping, how glad I was . . . then I suddenly loathed human beings once again, imprecated upon them and execrated them, I loathed human beings with all my vital energies, with my heart's entire capability of contempt, with the utmost urgency . . . so for a half an hour I ran all over the platform in the hope of making myself bearable to myself, but it was no use; I could not run away from myself; I am always running away from myself; that is of course the really horrible thing, that I am running away from myself and I cannot run away from myself . . . people term this condition despair . . . probably despair is unbearable when it reaches the point where one is trying to run away from oneself and cannot do so . . . at the same time, this condition is actually also the archetype of all destruction . . . you must make yourself realize that the centuries are incessantly assaulting one another in every human being, but nobody can withstand this condition, these constant eruptions, these monumental conceptual detonations, the convulsive agitation of the condition of competence . . . suddenly I made the discovery that I had left my book somewhere, that book about *The Unsearchable in Nature*, that book with the astonishingly highly sophisticated chapter about the ineptitude of nature that fundamentally transformed me over the course of the years; in fact, I thought, at some point I left this book lying somewhere, in this condition, on this journey, in this express train which was running more than an hour late and therefore had long since stopped deserving to be called an express train, you see; the people, the passengers should have been politely, graciously and self-evidently issued refunds at the destination; but can you really imagine that?—

that anything in our country would ever be done politely, graciously and self-evidently?; in fine and in short, I was obliged to go back to the dining car; the whole time I was wondering how I ever could have left behind the book, that dog-eared, muck-encrusted, completely broken-spined book whose very touch would have violently disgusted most people, all people; as this book invariably made such an appallingly foul impression, I was hopeful that I would find it again, that I would get it back; my hope had not been ill-founded; the book was still lying in its place; even though the dining car was now fully occupied, nobody had sat down at the table on which my book was lying, and, you see, I picked up the book, I took it into my custody, pressed it under my arm, and a couple of people immediately sat down at the table . . . but they are all of course sitting at a coffin, I thought; all the people here are sitting at a coffin and spooning up its contents, and the dining car itself is a coffin, and the people are all dressed for burial . . . in the waiters I incessantly beheld only pallbearers, only sweaty gravediggers . . . my mental image of this coffin on wheels was almost driving me crazy . . . so now I had my book back under my arm, and the people regarded me as crazy; suddenly I thought: yes, I am of course actually living in a horrible, physiognomic era! . . . and ran away; I stumbled over a row of crates and bottles and did not get involved in an altercation; an altercation was expected of me; I was even taken to task; I said that in all dining cars in the world the crates and bottles were stored in the corridors, in the narrow corridors intended for the exclusive use of passengers, which was horrible, I recall a series of contretemps in dining cars, never mind in which trains, never mind in which country ... in fine and in short, I was hiding inside myself, yet again, for the hundred-thousandth time I was hiding inside myself ... now the train was suddenly headed towards its destination at a speed faster than its allowable limit; I now saw in a single glance the small towns and villages being flung out the window, the trees bursting asunder, all to the accompaniment of the clattering of the maladroit cars, the tracks' cries of woe ... again I had been walking in the wrong direction; nothing but remarkably fatuous faces, foul-smelling crops of hair, an irreparable, instinctive, somnolent lovelessness ... above all, I was struck by the ghastly tastelessness of the men's neckties ... over time, I thought, everybody gets accustomed to this gruesome life that is going further and further out of its mind and getting further and further out of joint; they have long since drowned, suffocated in their own revolutionary youth ... an immeasurably repellent contentment, a boundless emotional and perceptual dullness swiftly spreads within individual characters and in the mass activities of human beings ... youth ultimately disavows its finest, its supremely intimate, its most supremely sensitive impulses, it eventually disavows even its own existence ... youth eventually becomes an analphabetic paragon of underdevelopment, and the adults usher it out of life, which now consists of nothing but compressed, toothless heads condemned to silence ... life, the old people say, is no longer worth talking about, and wherever one looks and wherever one goes, one sees: *life is no longer worth anything* ... in fact, I reached the end of the train; absorbed in these thoughts, quite simply *abstracted* into these thoughts, I all of a sudden found myself at the end of the train . . . as you know, that is quite a long train, the express train; indeed, I tell you, if I hadn't left my suitcase in the First Class compartment (my hat and my coat were also still in the compartment), I never would have walked back towards the front; but in fact, while walking back towards the front, I saw the young man; I remember it quite precisely; he squeezed past me; he wasn't wearing a coat, no, he wasn't; of course, I didn't see his shoes; in the narrow corridor I couldn't see any shoes; I was struck by the stubbiness of those arms of his; I only wanted to get by him quickly; his necktie was black, his shirt was filthy; I can remember it quite precisely; it was too tight for him, like the shirts of all these young people one encounters nowadays; his shirt was too tight, filthy and much too tight; he forced himself rather inconsiderately past me; all this lasted only a matter of seconds; naturally, I wasn't expecting an apology; indeed, he had shoved his arm into my back; he said something; I didn't understand it; no, there was no apology, no coat, and no hat on his head either, no hat; and immediately after that the train pulled into the station; all of a sudden, the light grew dim in the car, and I realized that I was in *my* car; indeed, I saw that I had encountered the man in front of *my* compartment; he had in truth given me the impression that he was a member of the intelligentsia; in fact, at that moment, he very much struck me as an intrinsically despairing and self-despair-ridden anarchistic, filthy worldling, as one of those deplorable great men of our age.

A Young Writer

Today I was prevented by the local police from making progress in my scientific work, and at the moment it even seems to me that thanks to their intervention every facet of this work has been destroyed; entire mountain ranges have vanished from the terra firma of my thought thanks to the uncouthness with which I was torn away from my books and papers and escorted to the police station; entire regions have been simply obliterated. As I was a half a year ago, I am once again like a man groping in the dark. My understanding is a hired servant of madness. In this handful of hours dictated to me by our melodramatic police, a colossal deterioration of my researches and my physics has occurred. —Their inquiry centres on the young writer who vanished several weeks ago and whom the public (the police) are implicating in the assassination of the foreign minister. It is a good thing that the man is finally dead, but it is ridiculous that the writer, the very person who immediately caused quite a sensation hereabouts

---

Originally published as 'Ein junger Schriftsteller' in 1965 in the Graz and Vienna-based literary journal *Wort in der Zeit*. [Trans. after Bernhard's editors]

with a handful of books, the author of *Sthenia* and *Asthenia*, is being associated with a political event, any sort of political event; that the foreign minister, the social-democratic scarecrow, is being associated with the thirty-year-old who wrote *The Forest in March*! The police interrogated me for more than two hours. The police harbour a colossal suspiciousness of people who think for themselves, an even more colossal suspiciousness of people who write their thoughts down and a downright appalling suspiciousness of people who publish their written thoughts, who make the public aware of them. The police harbour an especially great suspiciousness of writers. The written word is dreaded. I said regarding W. that his jacket was black, his head large, his hearing poor; then I said nothing further, nothing until my release two hours later and I thought: in point of exquisiteness of style, he is one of our greatest; his titles, because they are so short, are the best titles. At bottom, he is a philosophical mathematician. Reading aloud gave him no pleasure; he despised his listeners. He was surrounded by an overly numerous literary riffraff. He had written the loveliest letters, had the most horrible childhood. He was ill; I didn't know anything about the nature of his illness. This illness had made it difficult for him to count to a hundred and completely impossible for him to hurt a soul, and a man like this has supposedly killed the foreign minister . . . He had a predilection for analysing everything; he would go without speaking for weeks on end. Because his jacket was black, everybody must have supposed that he was coming straight from a funeral, or that he was going to a funeral, because his trousers were also black. He loathed hats. He loved newspapers, women of a vulnerable disposition, and children, children who ran around barefoot. He dreaded dogs and had a lifelong fear of catching a cold. In company, his unflagging taciturnity was conspicuous. He could give you a description of the various species of birds like nobody else and was well versed in physics and in the church liturgy. He was always talking about rowboats, never about material exigencies. He said that he always got his flashes of inspiration at night, that he wrote but read nothing. That he found friendships oppressive. That as the son of an organ builder he was especially knowledgeable about the preparation of rare woods and light metals. That he had very often managed to commit himself to his life of pure contentment but that his disposition had not allowed him to set foot in any refuge of any sort that had ever been offered to him. That nobody knew how widely he had travelled, that he was familiar with almost every European city and landscape; that he was acquainted with the most various, the most mutually antithetical sorts of people and he was making fewer and fewer errors in judgement. That he now had only so-called inner puzzles to solve; that he conceived of the external world as a body on which one could continually study the scabies afflicting nature in its entirety; that one could discover colossal modifications for nature's eczemas on its surface. That he was interested in 'a subterranean magic'. That he ultimately and fundamentally wished to analyse causes, not effects. That in places where the world was fantastical, he felt it emphatically, proximately, but that everywhere else he was repelled by it. That one person was nothing and the next person conceived of everything as an act of religious devotion. He spoke of the perseverance with which, unbeknownst to his intellect, he had lagged behind so long 'as if in an ulcerous prison of superficies' in his childhood and youth; he spoke of his 'beauteous, triumphant mindlessness'. He said that the most poignant moment in his life had been when out of the images that had seemingly surrounded him 'for millennia' he suddenly began making, crafting thoughts, in which humankind's greatest effort consists. Youth exists only in images; the average human being also exists only in images, not in thoughts; the average human being has never had a thought, and the same is true of the average so-called intellectual in his substandard, menial world; it is otherwise with the extraordinary individual who can engender thoughts and make and craft them in the extraordinary world. He said that he had no experience inasmuch as no human being had experience, not even an intuition of experience, that he had an intuition of the interstices of life, of the interstices in the nature of life. That he had been enamoured of certain walks he had taken and of certain people who had accompanied him on these walks, people with whom he had been able to express himself in a certain fashion. That he mediated conversations rather than carrying them on. At bottom, his participation in the world consisted in alluding to everything. Incapable of telling a story, he wrote better than anybody else of his generation, of his time, anybody else anywhere in Germany. His undemanding comportment surprised people as much as his congenital need to be demanding. He was also excessively proud. A streak of abusiveness towards his own person was discernible by everybody who encountered him. Time and again he maintained that he had no use for himself. Poverty depressed him and so did wealth. He was always sceptical in the presence of the slightest hint of good luck, which he described as pseudo-luck, a means of getting along, further and further along, a means of deceiving oneself and others from time to time. Not only did he wear black clothes on the outside, but also his inner world seemed to be lined with a shade of black that he had invented for that purpose. In his company, one could never allow oneself to feel sure of oneself on any subject; he could kill a person with every thought he formed. In every interlocution, he was accessible to the point of inaccessibility. It was as if he were surveying everything from a hunter's tower constituted by the darkness to which he alone had become accustomed in the course of his development, although it, this darkness, was slowly crushing him; this mechanism, this process, was clearly visible; one could observe this process; he saw through it as well, but only to the point of peering into the distances that left open his brain's aggregated tensional possibilities. From time to time, he would crawl away into the gloomiest valleys of our country, into the gloomiest civilizations. The displeasure of repeatedly being in the company of people who disgusted him, and most people disgusted him, was an adequate substitute for hundreds upon hundreds of books as far as he was concerned. Watercourses with wills of their own were great favourites of his, as were especially irritating, especially precise figures of speech. He had never alighted on desirability, only mediocrity. His lugubriousness was a manifestation of strength of will. At times, he seemed horrified by theories that he had suddenly discovered to be delusional constructions of his adversaries, of the people around him, of the world around him. He alleged to the world that he had never wished to behold it; if he had never been born, he said, he never would have needed to open his eyes! He said that his daily effort to rise 'above the rank and file and their greasiness, above their dimwittedness' had embittered him from a very early age. 'Oh, to be a dog or a cat!' he had often thought. One time, the last time we were walking through the city, I heard him say that he was a purposeless creature, but that human beings, and above all the masses, struck him as being equally purposeless. I, too, find from time to time that physical geography in its entirety gives me an impression of horrible purposelessness; every single day at street crossings one can observe the purposelessness of human beings, the purposelessness of nature. The only truly purposeful act consists in observing the purposelessness (of nature); thus do the philosophers and their philosophies grow old and thus does even science grow old with a colossal purposelessness! Purposelessness hisses and roars and it stinks and howls and is ravenous. Purposelessness is rampant in Europe and in all the other continents; the water is purposeless and the air is purposeless; everything material is purposeless. This purposelessness is persuasive. It is purposeless that anything exists; thoughts cannot think their way out of their purposelessness. I also walked with him through the woods one time, years ago; during that walk he had spoken in exactly the same way about how purposeless he was. If, he had said, *he* was purposeless, then *everything* was purposeless.

I understood immediately: he meant that the brainpower of the *in*competence of nature . . . the coarseness of those who are perfectly satisfied with their own purposelessness, of the whole heap of normal human beings, had repelled him and overawed him from his earliest childhood onwards. For a long time, three decades, 'three lethal decades', he had had the world and its enveloping atmosphere served up to him as an atmosphere deeply pregnant with meaning; he said that although he had always found this highly distressing, he had always spooned it up without demur. Suddenly he took a look at it and refused to continue assimilating it. The success he enjoyed seemed laughable to him. For him, the whole thing was nothing but a 'charade'. He marvelled at nothing. For a long time, it had even pained him that he was obliged to be *here*. Now, I thought (the interrogation had just ended, abortively ended), he has succeeded in achieving what he always desired. I asked myself where he was residing, but I could not imagine where he could be. So many places existed in my memory, but not a single one of them was right for him any longer. He no longer fitted into any town, into any city, into any territory, into any system. I tried to shift him at least into an imaginary landscape of familiarity, of constancy, but that didn't work either. He has killed himself; he has even *allegedly* killed himself. But they haven't found his body.

A Country Confidence Man

Having headed up the Danube out of fear of the Asian flu, we had got as far as the vicinity of Grein, where, taking advantage of this sudden supervention of reposefulness, the two of us made enormous strides in our work because, being both of a very highly disciplined bent, we were able to embark on the conclusion of our study entitled *Sylvicultura Oeconomica II.* At first, our attention was caught by an inn on the riverbank, an inn that was larger, more imposing, than any other we had ever seen, but that turned not to be not at all suitable for us, because we could not but presume that a large crowd of people would show up there each and every day and make a great deal of noise, especially in the evenings, when we are customarily thinking with the utmost concentration, to say nothing whatsoever of the interval between nine at night and one in the morning, which throughout our lives has always been highly precious to us. In fact, the very moment we set

---

Originally published in 1969 as 'Ein ländlicher Betrüger' in the first issue of *Ver Sacrum*, a revival of the Vienna Session's identically named magazine founded and edited by Otto Breicha, Georg Eisler and Bernhard's friend Hilde Spiel. [Trans. after Bernhard's editors]

foot in the inn's front-lawn orchard, a garden that delighted us with its embodiment of artistic and economic judgement in equally great measure, we immediately got the impression that here, albeit certainly not *right* here, there would always be people to disturb us, but we did not immediately turn around and leave the orchard to look for alternative lodgings, of which there were plenty in the area; rather, we stepped into the inn, into a vaulted foyer, into a spotless kitchen, into a pantry chock-full of victuals and potables from front to back. As our shouted queries as to whether anyone was at home were met with silence, we stepped back outside into the orchard, and from there we saw two men in blue overalls installing boundary stones alongside a brook. Immediately behind the two men stood a young man who was easy to identify as a surveyor. All surveyors look the same. He stood there and observed the two men whom he had condemned to absolute precision. We made our presence felt, and we were informed by the surveyor that the older of his two assistants was the landlord. The surveyor announced that he was a surveyor, but we did not say what our occupation was, because it is too unusual; we merely said that we were seeking lodgings, 'perfect but not sumptuous ones,' I said, naturally omitting to mention that we had left the capital for the Strudengau on account of the Asian flu; we also took pains to divert attention from our anxiousness, our circumspection in the presence of other people, in the presence of the possibility of illness; in any case, we took pains to seem uncomplicated, which is important in the country; one can never get anything done otherwise. A quiet, reposeful inn for one or two weeks, perfect working conditions, I said, adding that we had almost already completed a study, a rather lengthy work on the *byssus*. The surveyor was one of those condescending small-town dwellers one often encounters in the country, parochial even in his choice of clothing; the few words he uttered confirmed our judgement: that he was narrow-minded, petty, etc. . . . The landlord made an excellent first impression, as did his co-worker, an odd-job man from the village, as I now know. The surveyor addressed him as *Oswald*. The landlord said that his inn was quiet, that the food was good. But as he was saying that his inn was quiet, we both got the impression that in reality it was anything but quiet; when he said the food was good, we got the impression that we had reason to doubt that it was. Gradually—as we were conversing with the three of them (for we included the surveyor in the conversation) about the landscape, with which they were all intimately acquainted, as we immediately realized (even though it is also a complete mystery to them, just as we find it completely strange even though we are quite familiar with it); as we were conversing with them about the countryside, its people and its weather, as one always does, and thus conversing in a manner that is naturally ridiculous but also useful—we felt ourselves developing an ever-increasing aversion to the landlord, and also an aversion to Oswald the odd-job man, and an even greater aversion to the surveyor. We saw that the three of them were perfect examples of the class of people we abhor the most: men who are full-time urinal philosophers, funny face-pullers, baby-makers; sacrificial victims of an idyll fed exclusively by dimwittedness. We said that we were enthralled by the peculiarity of the region's geology, vegetation, etc.; that we were captivated by *salices*, *pyrolae*, *polyzonicae*, etc., and that we knew a thing or two about trees and plants, about hills and dales, about the composition of every possible type of air. A person could, I said, take a strong lifelong interest in the exploration of nature in its unblemished integrity, its internal as well as its external integrity. The three men had actually stopped working and started listening; I explained why and for what reasons the two of us thought of nature as a *musical score*. I explained that to peruse this score day in and day out was a habit, a passion for us. That *sickness* would be a better word for it. But the three of them understood none of it. They were living in the midst of nature and therefore did not understand it, etc. . . . Finally, I realized that it was pointless to keep speaking about something that was actually inexplicable; that was and is the truth, and I said that there was nobody indoors at the inn. That to step into an inn seeking relief of one's hunger and thirst and find no serving staff in attendance at all was vexatious, horrendous. It was really quite bizarre, I said, to leave an inn like this one completely unlocked, unattended, with all the doors and windows open, I said, but the landlord retorted that his wife was in the house, and that the barmaid was as well. He said that both of them were probably having a bath and not answering anybody because they were naked etc. . . . but as a matter of fact, he added, the barmaid was just then running through the beer garden, we looked over at it; two men were sitting at a table painted green, drinking beer, eating bacon. They're *also* strangers, said the landlord. He did not wait for our reaction;

he kept working, ordered Oswald to hammer a softwood post into the ground next to the boundary stone, and then took no further notice of us. The surveyor said nothing in reply to our parting salutation, whereas Oswald and the landlord saluted us in return. In the orchard, we soon found a shaded place to sit. We each ordered a beer, drained our glasses quickly, and ordered a second round, which, as if by way of securing our right to our table, we drank very slowly, more slowly than I had ever before drained a glass. We'll get a room in the small inn across the street; I like it immensely at first sight; it is uninviting, cold, always devoid of people, perfect for intellectual work, I thought, although I had already shifted my attention to the two men eating and drinking at the next table; one was about fifty years old and the other about seventy; both of them had white hair; the younger one obviously invited the older one to join him for a meal and the two have only just met each other, I thought; the vagrant has only just met the beggar and vice versa . . . the younger man had a grey jacket draped around his shoulders, the older man a black one around his; both of them were wearing un-ironed trousers; the clothing of the older man was torn, that of the younger man dirty but not torn; the younger man was wearing a necktie, the older man a collarless shirt; they were shod in black, rough-hewn boots. The younger man, the vagrant, was speaking with an Innviertel accent, the older man with a Mühlviertel one. The invitee was the listener, who was unmoved by the speaker's beneficence but humouring him on account of the costliness of the meal. The benefactor may have seen better times, I thought; he used to be a packing-list clerk in an agricultural warehouse, a secretary for a local council, a foreman at a gravel pit, etc. . . . every now and then he used a High German phrase; he kept saying the word *logarithm*. In front of him on the table lay his peaked cap, which, while no longer waterproof, still afforded good protection against the sun . . . he was sufficiently pretentious to be continually uttering the words *infanta* and *Byzantinism*, which the beggar did not understand at all, and to be constantly talking about his sister who was married to a lawyer in Schlierbach, to be incessantly talking about rich relatives that he said he had wherever he went, and he said he went everywhere; he said these relatives even included a prelate and an abbot in a lower-Austrian monastery, indeed, even a cobblestone-pavement manufacturer . . . He said his listener was to eat whatever he liked and whatever he was in the mood for. The vagrant encouraged the beggar to eat (and drink) as many things as possible, and the beggar ate as many types of food as possible and drank as many types of drink as possible. I thought we should sit in the beer garden for another quarter of an hour and then secure our lodgings at the inn across the way; we'll step into that spooky inn, I thought, and go into a room and lay the manuscript of *Sylvicultura Oeconomica II* on a table, etc. . . . and then take a walk; our prospective destination was a basilica. It would have been a shame to get back up right away, because the vagrant and the beggar were worth observing further; I was once again deriving a series of important conclusions from my observation of them . . . The vagrant was from Hellmonsödt, his listener a native of Enns. The man from Hellmonsödt was talking; the man from Enns was listening. The topic of all this talking and listening was a life that was described as pitiful and yet not a jot more pitiful than fantastical, an equally pitiful and fantastical world for which the speaker thought one had to pay a price that was always much too high whether one liked it or not . . . 'Eat! Drink!' said the vagrant, and the beggar ate and drank. We had long since aroused the generous man's attention. All of a sudden, he said, 'Yes, yes, the Asian flu . . . ,' and he added that we were obviously from the city, and in flight from that horrible disease that stirs up terror everywhere just like the plague . . . but I had no desire to converse with the man and made no reply. We uttered some remarks about *foeminae*. An entire chapter about the *korm* worms, I said. The vagrant opined that it was not Asiatic flu alone that came from the city, fanned out over the entire countryside, etc., that history proved that all devastation, all misfortune, came from the city. He evinced unqualified contempt for city people. 'Music, dance, opera, revolution,' he said: 'they're all drivel.' To the beggar he said he should eat his fill, that it was a once-in-a-lifetime opportunity to be treated by somebody from Hellmonsödt, that it would never be repeated under any circumstances. Suddenly, the benefactor leapt to his feet; he said he had to go to the toilet. The beggar followed the vagrant with his eyes as he walked to the toilet. He had taken his peaked cap with him . . . A half an hour later, the man from Hellmonsödt had still not come back from the toilet. We observed the beggar, who, as he continued to eat with ever-increasing uneasiness, kept his eyes fixed on the door through which the man who had invited him to eat and drink so much was supposed to return to the table. A short time later—after going to the other inn, at which we secured our room and intended to stay and above all to work (to this day, we retain the fondest remembrance of both the stay and the work!) for a couple of days—on a street that we would have to cross if we wanted to get to the basilica, we saw the man from Hellmonsödt (but perhaps he was from some completely different place?) getting into a car that he had just flagged down and then riding off in it. We thought about the beggar still sitting in the beer garden at that moment, still waiting for the vagrant who had long since totally and permanently vanished, and probably still eating and drinking to calm himself, and the situation in which the beggar now found himself gradually became clear to us.

As an Administrator at the Asylum: A Fragment

Suddenly in connection with a crime, I read, people must have an alibi for a day about which they no longer know anything at all, no longer can know anything; with a feeling of certainty I think: this horrifies me; hundreds of thousands of people, merely on account of their forgetfulness regarding a specific day, and hence in many cases a literally *lethal* day, are persecuted by the judiciary and incarcerated for years, for decades, indeed, for life; one should not believe that prisons are populated only by the guilty; probably there are more innocent people than guilty ones in the prisons; how many innocent people have been executed, I think, and then I think: what was I doing last Friday, on the Saturday before last, or two Tuesdays ago, three Mondays ago, or for example on the day I turned thirty-four? . . . I no longer even know what I did yesterday, to say nothing of the day before yesterday . . . suddenly a person is expected to remember what he was

---

Originally published in 1970 as 'Als Verwalter im Asyl. Fragment' in Vol. 12 of the West German intellectual review *Merkur*. [Trans. after Bernhard's editors]

doing on the thirty-first of April* 1967, today, three years later . . . this certainly makes a mockery of the judiciary, but at the same time, it makes many of these people into some of the most unfortunate people one can imagine . . . a person who does not know today what he was doing on the thirty-first of April 1967, can, as I read, be sentenced to twenty years of deprivation of liberty, in other words, imprisonment, I think during breakfast, while they are talking . . . I am silent, because I have made a habit of being silent during breakfast; they are talking during breakfast, because they have made a habit of talking during breakfast . . . they talk uninterruptedly while they are eating their breakfast, whereas I think, whereas I am uninterruptedly silent while they are eating their breakfast, while I am thinking . . . it is the most depressing thing in the world, I think, to think about the judiciary, there is absolutely nothing more depressing than thinking about the judiciary; every day during breakfast I think about the judiciary, I no longer ever manage *not* to have to think about the judiciary during breakfast . . . and what is more I would probably be the most fortunate of human beings if I no longer had to think about the judiciary, if I were at least completely indifferent to everything having anything whatsoever to do with the judiciary . . . I think: they are talking, whereas you are being silent; by turns I think about the judiciary, and I think with ever greater intensity about the judiciary, about the thousands

* *Sic* on the nonexistent date, to which Bernhard seems to have had a peculiar partiality: On 22 February 1981, he wrote to his publisher, Siegfried Unseld, 'I wish to publish . . . a book that I shall deliver on 31 April, if this is all right with you!!!' [Trans.]

and hundreds of thousands of judicial *errors*, about this enormous multi-millennially ancient judicial *catastrophe* . . . What does it mean for there to be a judicial *error*! and what does it mean to be innocent and incarcerated and to have to sit innocently for days and years and decades in our horrible prisons . . . I think about this incredible judicial *anachronism* that nobody ever brings up for debate . . . you are uninterruptedly thinking, whereas they are uninterruptedly talking, I think, and then I think: to think that they are talking and that you are thinking and that they are eating and that you are eating and that they are not allowing their eating to be disturbed and that you are not allowing your thinking to be disturbed; to think that they are eating with ever greater intensity and that you are thinking with ever greater intensity, and that you, as you are thinking and as they are eating, are all of a sudden becoming preoccupied with the connection between your thinking and their eating and between your silence and their talking and between your art of thinking and their art of eating and between their dilettantism in eating and between* your dilettantism in thinking . . . becoming preoccupied with what sort of connection subsists between your thinking about the judiciary and their eating, between judicial errors and their cheap, defective clothing, between your loathing of our mindless laws and your loathing of our mindless authorities, between your loathing of the judiciary and you loathing of *their* pitifulness, with what sort of connection subsists between their constant voracity and your loathing of the judiciary . . .

* This illogical repetition of 'between' (*zwischen*), like the one preceding 'the municipal council' on p. 200, occurs in the original story.

to think that it all boils down to a completely degenerate judiciary on the one hand and completely degenerate people on the other, to rotten and tattered people's rotten and tattered shoes and rotten and tattered people's rotten and tattered laws; to think that there subsists a connection between judicial feeblemindedness and asylal feeblemindedness that must not be ignored . . . a connection between criminality and the spooning up of breakfast soup by the inmates of asylums, between the national government and between the municipal council responsible for the asylum, between the legislators of the judiciary and the legislators of the rules of the asylum, between the judiciary's jails and prisons on the one hand and the nursing homes and asylums on the other . . . to think that the regulations in the prisons and in the asylums are plainly and simply the same as the regulations in the jails and in the nursing homes, that the judiciary may be effortlessly likened to the elderly hunched over their soup bowls, that, indeed, these two things, the judiciary and the elderly, the judiciary and the soup bowls, the judiciary and the spoons and the voracity with which these spoons spoon up the soup, are identical to each other . . .

The Woman from the Foundry and the Man with the Rucksack

The woman who is employed at the foundry happened to notice an elderly man who, with a fully packed rucksack, was pacing up and down the riverbank, a man who was wearing deerskin trousers tied up at the ankles, a pair of thick-soled lace-up boots, a coat made of milled cloth and a sturdy felt hat on his head. She thought there was something terrifying about the face of the man, who seemed, like her, to be impatiently awaiting the arrival of the train, this man who now and then would quite unwarrantably shove another person out of the way in order to keep his own path clear. Even before getting to the train stop, she had observed the man and begun forming thoughts about him. The man was a complete stranger to her. He also was a stranger to her male and female co-workers, who on the way to the stop had successively asked her about him

---

Originally published as 'Eine Frau aus dem Gußwerk und der Mann mit dem Rucksack' in 1970 in the Wuppertal-based annual *Almanach 4 für Literatur und Theologie*. The story was Bernhard's response to repeated requests for a contribution to the volume from the person responsible for it, the literary critic Jürgen P. Wallmann. [Trans. after Bernhard's editors]

in the most unobtrusive fashion and invariably by means of the same question: *who is he*? Most people can be quite easily identified, classified, via their clothing, via their hats and coats and footwear; what a person is wearing immediately attests to where he comes from. The foundry's employees are immediately identifiable, as are the warehouse staff, the woodcutters, the day-trippers from the city, brewery workers, railwaymen, postmen, miners. But the man with the unusual felt hat on his head, with the unusually thick-soled lace-up boots, the man with the coat of sturdy milled fabric, with the deerskin leather trousers tied together at the ankles and *not under the knees*, was irritating. And to a most appalling degree he irritated the woman from the foundry, who suddenly, and while beckoning to several of her male and female co-workers, walked up to within a pace of the man and ordered him to open his rucksack. The stranger, completely surprised by her super-suddenness, opened his rucksack in the light of her ominousness and invasiveness and her ultimately unmistakable suspiciousness of him, and the woman from the foundry peered into the bag. The woman raised her head in disappointment, and the man with the rucksack stopped holding his breath. The rucksack had contained nothing but a rolled-up Hubertus coat. At this moment, the train pulled up to the stop. The foundry-workers climbed aboard; the woman from the foundry climbed aboard as well. In the poorly lit and overheated train, she tried to find a seat as far away as possible from the strange man who was carrying the rucksack that she was already beginning to find sinister again.

Lowlands

If we had ever been informed of and thereby enlightened in a tremendous fashion about the fact that our life process is in truth nothing but a pathological process—we tell ourselves and ask ourselves, *what*, or rather, *who* has not informed us of it and not enlightened us about it to any extent whatsoever; we tell ourselves and ask ourselves this over and over again and always while levelling the same, the ever-same, allegations against our parents as well as against our entire social environment in which, as we now see, we were compelled to exist for decades without ever actually seeing and hence for decades without ever actually thinking; above all, we ask ourselves *why our parents* never informed us and therefore enlightened us, when it was after all their duty (as we now believe, and as we are well within our rights to believe) to inform us and enlighten us and above all, as we know, to inform us and enlighten us regarding the fact that our life-process is nothing

---

Originally published in 1973 as 'Ebene' by the Salzburg-based firm Residenz in the artist Walter Pichler's collection *111 Zeichnungen. Mit einem Essay von Max Peintner und einem Prosatext von Thomas Bernhard.* Pichler designed some of the covers of Bernhard's books published by Residenz. [Trans. after Bernhard's editors]

but a pathological process and consequently has always been nothing but a pathological process, a fact that is immediately recognizable as a fact of nature—we would in those informed and enlightened circumstances have relinquished everything and abandoned everything much earlier and actually would have left behind everything for ever; decades ago, we would gone away—and would have gone down—and also would have gone out of ourselves—we would have gone down and would have relinquished and abandoned and left behind and extinguished* everything. Now, to our horror, we are beholding the ruthlessness and the vulgarity and the dimwittedness of our parents, by whom we, because they are our parents, were never enlightened to any extent whatsoever about the fact that our life process is in truth a pathological process, because our parents always hid their understanding from us, as we are now learning much too late. Had we been thus enlightened, then we would, we think, have gone out of ourselves decades ago and would have gone down and would have abandoned everything and left behind everything; we would have been obliged to do what we are doing now back then, decades ago; obliged to go away, to abandon, to leave behind, to extinguish, such that decades ago we would have been effortlessly able to put up with and put behind us what

---

* *Gone down* (*hinuntergegangen*) ... the first of several instances in this story of *Hinuntergehen*, a variant of the key Bernhardian concept of *Untergehen-Untergang* (see p. 53 footnote in 'The Decline of the West'); *extinguished* (*ausgelöscht*): an instance of another key concept in Bernhard's work: *Auslöschung*, which serves as the title of Bernhard's last-published novel, known in English as *Extinction*. [Trans.]

is now causing us to strain and overtax ourselves in the most extreme and humiliating fashion; what we now regard as an atrocity and not only an atrocity against everything, but also quite simply an atrocity against nature in its entirety, what we now regard as lies, we would have regarded as nothing but a part of our development, of our education; what we now find nothing but lethal we would have regarded as ideation. Had we been thus enlightened, we would not now in full knowledge of our causes be at the mercy of our effects in the most degrading fashion; had we been thus enlightened, we would not have done what we have done and would not be what we are. Decades ago, we would have gone out of ourselves and have gone away and gone down and would have abandoned everything and left behind everything: our walls and our furniture and the air in these walls and in these pieces of furniture and our books and our papers and the air in these books and in these papers, which have always been our books and our papers and which, as we now see, have also always been lethal walls and lethal furniture and a lethal air. Our lethal parents, we think, and we think that decades ago we ought to have relinquished everything and abandoned everything and left behind everything and extinguished everything in which we have been imprisoned for whole decades, and we have not only been imprisoned in this horribleness but also been exhausted from the very beginning and, as we now see, imprisoned in uninterrupted and persistent and ultimately insistent exhaustion thanks to our lethal parents. Many decades ago, we ought to have relinquished what we can no longer relinquish and abandon and leave behind and no longer can extinguish even if we go away and if we abandon and leave behind and extinguish, because we no longer have the strength for this, because our exhaustion is a total exhaustion. Decades ago, we could have calmly abandoned these walls and abandoned these pieces of furniture and relinquished these books and papers and shut these doors and exhaled our last breath of this air to avoid having to inhale a single breath ever again and to be able to forget everything, as we can now no longer do. We have relinquished and abandoned and left behind and forgotten what we believed we had to relinquish, abandon and leave behind and ultimately forget; we have gone out of ourselves and we have gone away and we have gone down by coming down here, but we have relinquished nothing and abandoned nothing and left nothing behind and forgotten nothing; we have in reality extinguished nothing whatsoever, because our parents never informed us of or enlightened us about the fact that our life process is in reality nothing but a pathological process. We used to be up there, in the company of our parents, locked up in our walls and in our rooms and in our books and papers and everything around us and in us was nothing but lethal, and now we are down here, without our parents, and once again we are locked up in these walls of ours and in our rooms and in our books and papers and everything around us and in us is nothing but lethal.